The Seventeen Dollar Murders

A Boomer/Senior Mystery

Melinda Richarz Lyons

The Seventeen Dollar Murders

©2018 by Melinda Richarz Lyons

All rights reserved.

ISBN: 978-1-61752-202-4
TreasureLine Publishing

Cover Design/Interior Design by Tell~Tale Book Covers

Also available in eBook publication

PRINTED IN THE UNITED STATES OF AMERICA

To my very own Ex and lifelong friend, Eddie

Thanks to my sister Charisse for her editing expertise

One

The Beatles' *Twist and Shout* jarred Rose Ellen from a dream about dancing with the Fab Four in the rain. She fumbled for her smart phone on the coffee table, wondering who had the nerve to disturb her afternoon nap and a dream where she had displayed some great dance moves.

She yawned at the sound of her best friend Pearl's voice. Rose Ellen had been divorced from Pearl's brother for several years. Despite the sometimes-awkward family dynamics, the two had remained closer than sisters.

When questioned about the unusual relationship between ex-sisters-in-law, Rose Ellen would quip, "I didn't divorce Pearl. I only divorced her brother."

"What is so important, Pearl?"

"Hey, Ex." The nickname Pearl used for Rose Ellen often drew odd looks from strangers when they were together. "Are you watching TV?"

"No. I was enjoying a siesta with Oscar."

Rose Ellen looked at her still sleeping orange tabby with envy. He had only opened one eye momentarily, when he heard the Beatles ringtone.

"Well, turn it on! There's breaking news!"

"What's wrong, Pearl?" Rose Ellen asked, as she reached for the TV remote.

"What's wrong? There's been another murder, that's what's wrong! That makes three! What in the Sam Hill is going on?"

"Wait a minute. Let me back it up, so I get the whole story."

Rose Ellen watched in disbelief as the newscaster described a third, eerily similar murder in as many months. All three victims had been left in almost identical positions and were women over sixty.

The first victim had been found behind a boarded-up Foley's store, while the second was discovered in an abandoned Walmart parking lot. The latest had been left in a field just outside of town.

"They are calling them the Seventeen Dollar Murders," Pearl said.

"I know. This is getting scary. Why would someone do something so brutal and then leave a ten-dollar bill, plus a five and two ones at the crime scene?"

"It has to mean something. I bet they don't find any fingerprints at this murder scene, either. Just like the last two. And to think this is happening in our little town, Ex. Well…"

Rose Ellen interrupted, "I know the police have tried, but there seems to be nothing to go on."

Their hometown wasn't little, like it had been in the sixties. It had boomed into an area that included almost one hundred thousand souls, but most residents still described it as a place with small town charm.

Like any city, Tyler had its share of crime, but ones like the recent gruesome homicides were rare. Three older women had been found strangled, stabbed and left holding seventeen dollars. That was something you read about happening in New York City or Chicago.

Tucked in the East Texas piney woods, Tyler was

normally laid back and quiet. Multi-colored roses and azaleas lined the brick streets downtown, and you couldn't go more than a few blocks without passing a church steeple, a barbecue joint or a store that sold both guns and guitars.

For the most part, people in Tyler still lived by the golden rule and believed in southern hospitality, being neighborly and using the "it takes a village" approach to parenting.

Northern folks might consider some things about East Texas residents quirky, like the fact that women generally didn't go to their mailboxes without full makeup, and most men would say that their favorite color was camouflage. But behind the pine curtain, that was normal.

"What on earth is happening, Pearl?"

"I don't know. Used to be the worst thing that happened was a 7-Eleven robbery. But this goes way beyond that. What really scares me is that they are targeting women like us."

Both born and raised in East Texas, Rose Ellen and Pearl enjoyed flaunting that with their matching t-shirts purchased on sale at the local Cracker Barrel. The shirts read "GRITS" for "Girls Raised in the South."

They welcomed newcomers to the Lone Star state, but couldn't resist kidding the ones from colder climates with phrases like, "Nobody retires and moves up north."

Proud of its history, the women loved to share stories with transplants about their state's colorful past, and brag about how everything really was bigger and better in Texas. They delighted in pointing out examples, like the fact that the famous South Texas King Ranch was larger than the state of Rhode Island.

The two baby boomers had grown up with Roy Rogers, backyard bomb shelters, *Leave it to Beaver*, hula hoops and ballerina dolls. Misbehaving was nothing more than hiding under the covers after bedtime, with a flashlight and a copy of the latest Nancy Drew book. And they never phoned a boy, unless it was to call him back.

Rose Ellen and Pearl idolized Annette Funicello and practiced dancing like the kids on *American Bandstand* and *Shindig!* at slumber parties. Their teenage years were spent perusing the pages of *Seventeen* for the latest fashions and fads, and spending their babysitting money on 45s.

They caught the tail end of Elvis's meteoric rise to stardom and listened to everything from The Four Tops and Rolling Stones, to The Beach Boys and Beatles on their transistor radios.

Sack dresses, circle pins and Ben Casey blouses gave way to tie dyed shirts, peace symbols and Cher hair. Both women went to college to become teachers and land a man.

High school friends before they became kin, the retired educators had raised their children together and supported each other during a lot of challenging times, like their kids' turbulent teenage years.

Rose Ellen discovered the true strength of their friendship after she left Pearl's brother. She supported all of Rose Ellen's choices, even when the newly divorced Rose Ellen decided to downsize and move into a tiny house in a "seniors only" village.

Other friends had questioned her decision, but

Rose Ellen loved the fact that her tiny house did not require much maintenance, and she could enjoy a pool she didn't have to clean. It was also wonderfully quiet living in a place that didn't allow any residents under fifty-five.

Tyler's Tiny House Village was small compared to the movement in Spur, Texas, where the town had encouraged people from all over the country to come to "the old west town that welcomes new pioneers."

Still, Rose Ellen found the village friendly, safe and comfortable. She also enjoyed amenities like the lawn care service and clubhouse, where various social groups often gathered.

Pearl was grateful for Rose Ellen's support after her husband died suddenly. Friends who weren't widows had abandoned her, because she wasn't part of a couple anymore. But her ex-sister-in-law's friendship never wavered.

The two spent their days playing Forty-Two, attending potlucks and church socials. They helped with library events, like the annual book sale and various senior fund raisers, including the Senior Follies Talent Show.

They both loved crime shows on the Investigation Discovery network and had even signed up online to be ID Addicts. The duo could discuss topics like forensics for hours.

Neither had much interest in dating, but both were country music fans. They often went to boot scooting dances at the Tyler Senior Society. The two were also members of a line dancing group that performed at local assisted living centers and nursing homes.

Their town was often referred to as the Rose

Capital of the United States, because it was home to the nation's largest rose garden. The colorful Texas Rose Festival celebrated the abundance of homegrown flowers and drew thousands of tourists to Tyler every October.

It was a great place for active seniors. With three major medical facilities and cutting edge care available, Tyler had become a mecca for retirees. There was a plethora of activities and organizations that catered to the growing population, including an annual Senior Expo, Seniors Celebrating Life events and the East Texas State Fair Boomers and Seniors Day.

Rose Ellen and Pearl took full advantage of all their retirement town had to offer, particularly the fact that most shops and restaurants offered senior discounts.

Like a lot of people their age, Rose Ellen and Pearl often found it hard to grasp the idea that their generation of postwar baby boomers had either already joined the ranks of seniors, or were soon to be classified as senior citizens. But that was okay, because the same kids who rebelled with rock and roll and protest marches, were luckily, rebelling against aging.

After all, age was just a number. No matter what the calendar said, the two vowed to stay active and live each day as if it were their last. And the charming town in East Texas was a perfect place to stay engaged and young at heart.

It was also inspiring to be surrounded by older seniors who refused to give in to rocking chairs. Their friend Peggy was a great example of that.

Her "never too old to have fun" attitude made her a popular figure with men and women. She had celebrated her ninetieth birthday on the Senior Society's dance floor with Chubby Checker. Peggy rocked and rolled as *Come on Baby, Let's Do the Twist* blared from the computerized sound system.

She certainly had her share of aches and pains and had experienced a lot of tragedy in her life. But Peggy never complained and greeted everyone with an optimistic smile. She often voiced her philosophy, "Stand tall, wear an invisible crown and be as sweet and soft as divinity on the inside."

Rose Ellen and Pearl had a lot of fun friends. They did enjoy each other's company, but weren't joined at the hip. Rose Ellen had her quilting group and interest in reading. She particularly liked mysteries and romance novels featuring older women, the genre fashionably referred to as "boomer lit."

Pearl loved to work out and could often be found on weekday mornings at a senior water aerobics class in the Olympic-size pool at the Tyler Y.M.C.A.

Generally, life was good and their golden years were happy and tranquil, except now-- with three unsolved, brutal murders.

"Why are they after women our age? There is no evidence that robbery was involved, and there doesn't seem to be a sexual aspect to the crimes. I just can't understand the motive. And it might be the same killer."

"You're right," Rose Ellen responded. "But then like that guy said the other night on the show about all those homicides in Ohio, we can't possibly understand the criminal mind."

"I know, Ex. But what would make someone do that, and what is the significance of the seventeen dollars in cash? Or was the money left just to throw the police off track?"

"I have no idea." Rose Ellen turned off the TV and plopped down next to a still snoozing Oscar on the couch. "I sure hope they are able to solve these crimes quickly, before the killer strikes again."

The two discussed the fact that the homicides seemed like overkill. According to news reports, the victims had probably been stabbed after they had been strangled to death. Each method was personal and emotional, but together they indicated a very angry killer—a killer who wanted to punish three older women. But why?

"I can't help thinking about the fact that they were all baby boomers. That has to mean something. Maybe the police need some help figuring this out."

"Pearl, what are you talking about? They have crime labs that can test the most minute amount of DNA, and there is the CODIS data base to see if a person's DNA is in the system. There are even profilers these days that can get real close to the personality traits of a specific killer."

"But they don't have much to go on. Just those bills. From what I understand, they have no hair or blood evidence. They must be missing something. Maybe we can help."

Rose Ellen dropped her smart phone. It bounced off the Yeti tumbler resting on the coffee table and landed on her sleeping feline. Oscar jumped up and let out a disgusted "Meow."

She retrieved it and shouted into the phone, "Are

you nuts?"

"We have learned a thing or two watching all the crime shows. You know, I have been thinking about where the victims were found and if there is a connection with the locations."

"Come on, Pearl. Watching sixty-minute crime shows does not qualify us to solve a string of murders. I'm sure the cops have already considered the possible significance of the locations."

"I know. But maybe, because we are amateurs, so to speak—we could see things from a different perspective."

Rose Ellen was used to Pearl's goofy ideas, but this was beyond goofy. It was downright ridiculous, or as they said in the South, "That's as crazy as a pet raccoon."

Pearl had done some off the wall things in the past. One time, at a Senior Society dance, Pearl had convinced a would-be suitor that she was a retired homicide detective, and her hobby was looking at crime scene photos.

When Rose Ellen scolded her about telling lies, Pearl had defended herself by saying that was her way of discouraging him.

"Well, you could have just told him you weren't interested," Rose Ellen had said at the time, knowing that would not have been flashy enough for Pearl.

Then, there was the incident at the Tiny House Village swimming pool when Pearl decided a midnight skinny dip might be fun. Luckily, Rose Ellen had convinced her that no one in the entire Lone Star State would find saggy, wrinkled skin appealing--even in the soft moonlight.

Not only was Rose Ellen used to Pearl's crazy ideas and behavior, she kind of enjoyed them. Being much more reserved, she got a kick out of Pearl's more flamboyant personality. But this—this was too much.

"Now, Pearl, you've had some questionable ideas in the past, like that time you thought we should sign up for belly dancing at our ages. But..."

"That wasn't questionable," Pearl interrupted. "I would have done it. You were the chicken."

"That's not being a chicken! I was just being reasonable. We don't exactly have the bodies for belly dancing. I didn't have any desire to show off my poochy, old stomach. And that's what I'm saying now. Be reasonable. Two seniors—even aficionados of the ID network--cannot solve murders that are challenging our local police force. It is as simple as that."

"Sometimes, you and your reasonable self are just no fun. I think we could crack the cases wide open if we just gave it a try."

Rose Ellen sighed. "I don't think that's likely."

"Don't rule out the possibility that we could do some investigating. We could call ourselves the boomer/senior sleuths."

Rose Ellen bit her tongue. It was best not to argue. Sometimes that just fueled the fire with Pearl. Time to change the subject, she thought.

She glanced at the clock above her kitchen sink. That was one of the best things about living in a one level tiny house. Everything was compact. She could see what time it was from any angle, spot who was at the door from her bedroom, and cleaning was a breeze.

"Hey, Pearl, it's almost three and the potluck starts at four."

"Oh, I nearly forgot. I already made my cranberry salad. I just have to grab it from the frig."

Rose Ellen looked at the store-bought cookies from Brookshire Brothers Grocery on her little kitchen counter and cringed. Her mother would not approve, but then her mother never had to cook in a pint-sized kitchen.

"You know red-hair-from-a-bottle Ruth will bring something that everybody loves. Then when we want the recipe, she will leave out an ingredient. That way nobody can make it as good as she does."

"You're right, but Ruth is not the only one that does that, Pearl. What about dumb Nelda? She actually left the chicken off the recipe card for her so-called famous chicken casserole."

Nelda was well known in senior circles for showing up on every new widower's door step—casserole in hand—sometimes before funeral arrangements had been made. It was a move that many grieving relatives did not appreciate. Her gestures had also been unsuccessful, since she was still single.

"Guess she didn't think about that. Should have left out a spice or something. At least it wouldn't have been quite so obvious," Pearl added.

"She's not the brightest bulb in the chandelier, to say the least." Rose Ellen could not help gritting her teeth when it came to any conversation about Nelda. Her hatred went way back to their high school days.

Nelda had done everything she could to come between Rose Ellen and her then boyfriend and future husband. Nelda even stole a kiss from him on the dance floor the night of their senior prom at John Tyler High School.

Since the marriage didn't end well, Rose Ellen often thought about what life would have been like if she had just allowed Nelda to steal her high school crush. But then--without that relationship, she might not have her daughter, Jennifer.

She resisted voicing anything negative about the final, unhappy years of her marriage to Pearl. Rose Ellen appreciated Pearl's friendship enough not to openly express distasteful thoughts about her brother. It was one of the few topics they never discussed.

The friction between Rose Ellen and Nelda may have started on prom night, but it didn't end there. At every available opportunity, Nelda had flirted shamelessly with Rose Ellen's husband.

Too bad her ex-husband moved out of town, Rose Ellen thought. Now, Nelda could shamelessly flirt with him all she wanted.

"Nelda's not only dumb, she's also as ugly as homemade soap. The worst part is—she doesn't even realize that," Pearl said, knowing that would make her best friend's tight jaw turn into a big grin.

Rose Ellen let out a little giggle and replied, "Well, if the boot fits…"

Calling a person stupid or ugly was something both women considered cruel. But Nelda was an exception.

Rose Ellen knew better than to ask Pearl what she would be wearing to the potluck. Her taste in clothes was as flamboyant as her personality. It wasn't unusual for her to show up in a tight, neon green top from Forever 21. Apparently, she took that literally, like the aging lioness who looked in the mirror and saw a kitten.

Unlike Pearl, Rose Ellen was more of a "forever 61" fashionista. She didn't wear baggy, granny clothes, but preferred to don flattering styles that were age appropriate.

"Will thirty minutes give you enough time to get ready?"

"Sure. I'm already dressed. I found these really cute leggings on sale. I'm gonna wear those."

Oh, great, thought Rose Ellen. Her ex-sister-in-law was going to make another grand entrance in something that looked like it came from her granddaughter's closet. This time, leggings--and maybe a matching tank top. Pearl would certainly stand out in a room full of long, loose blouses and neatly pressed, dark slacks. Maybe that was the point.

"Sounds good, Ex. We can pig out and chat. I want to hear about your quilting club."

Rose Ellen hung up and blew out a sigh. She knew Pearl didn't want to talk about quilting. She might start the conversation with a few questions about Rose Ellen's latest project, but more than likely, she would quickly turn it into a discussion about how two old ladies from the piney woods of East Texas could solve a series of baffling, brutal murders.

Two

Rose Ellen was just about to pull out of her small, attached carport, when she saw a neighbor with his little Yorkie in tow. He knocked on the driver's window, and Rose Ellen reluctantly rolled it down.

Kenny had only lived in the Tiny House Village a few months. The move was prompted by the death of his wife several years earlier. He told Rose Ellen that he wanted to find a fresh start in his new home.

The problem was he had apparently decided his fresh start only included Rose Ellen. He didn't seem to have many visitors, and he rarely participated in any of the village or local Senior Society activities.

Although she had constantly encouraged him to be more outgoing, Rose Ellen was beginning to feel like her suggestions were falling on deaf ears. It was becoming more difficult to be nice to a man who thought she was his only social outlet.

"Oh hey, Kenny. I am running a little late for the potluck. Wanna come? There will be plenty of food," she asked, praying that he would turn her down. She was getting tired of babysitting for an older man who acted like a small child.

"No. I don't have anyone to make anything. It would be so sad without Bess, too."

Rose Ellen shoved the cookies under her purse on the seat, so Kenny wouldn't get any ideas about jumping in her car and running down to Brookshire Brothers Grocery to pick up something.

"Well, maybe next time."

"When will you be back?"

She tried to think quickly, so he wouldn't suggest another night watching TV--which meant listening to Kenny talk over whatever show was on.

She felt badly for him, but it was frustrating to deal with someone who did not want to help himself. He seemed to prefer wallowing in his misery and trying to drag Rose Ellen down with him.

"I don't know, Kenny. I am picking Pearl up, and then we might do something after, like go shopping for shoes."

Maybe that would do it. She couldn't picture Kenny looking at cute shoes with two graying women.

"Okay," he mumbled. "Maybe tomorrow night."

"I will let you know," she said as she rolled up the window. She gave him a weak wave and backed out.

Rose Ellen had never felt any romantic vibes from Kenny. He was just lonely, she thought. But still—she could not be responsible for his happiness. Dealing with him occasionally was fine, but she had to put a stop to his nightly visits. He could get out and rejoin the world, too, just like she did after her divorce.

Maybe if she wasn't as available, it would push him to find his own entertainment. Then she might be able to suggest he try something like the Seniors Singles Night at Brookshire Brothers. They always had good attendance and lots of free food samples.

Maybe not, she thought, as she pictured him boring some poor, unsuspecting widow with photos of his dead wife. She felt a little guilty, but a mental image of Kenny trapping some helpless woman near the fresh cantaloupes and watermelons from the South

Texas valley, made her chuckle.

Pearl was waiting in her driveway when Rose Ellen came roaring up. She hated to be late. In fact, Pearl preferred to be early everywhere they went.

"Now Pearl, we have more than enough time," Rose Ellen assured her, trying to fend off Pearl's usual complaints about being late. "I got waylaid by Kenny."

"Again? You are nicer than I am. I would tell him to get lost."

"I just don't know if I can be that blunt."

"Sure, you can, Ex. I know he suffered a loss, but so have a lot of people our age. He is just playing on your sympathy. Besides, it's been a while since he lost his wife. You know, what you are doing is called enabling. You need to cut him loose, and then he'll be forced to deal with life again."

Pearl knew firsthand how difficult it was to lose a spouse. It hadn't been easy, but she had crawled out of that dark tunnel of grief and taken the initiative to rebuild her life.

Based on her own experiences, grief counseling, bereavement books and watching *Dr. Phil*, Pearl's advice was right on.

Kenny would not stop depending on Rose Ellen for emotional support and social contact, until she put an end to it. It was time for Kenny to move forward and away from her.

"Hey, I've got an idea," Pearl giggled.

"Let's give his address to Nelda. She would chase him so hard he would either run like a jackrabbit, or end up eating homemade casseroles every night."

The two were laughing hysterically as they rounded the corner to the tree-lined street that welcomed them to the Tyler Senior Society building.

Pearl flipped the visor down and checked her lipstick in the mirror. She reached into her purse and touched up her already brightly colored lips.

Rose Ellen wished she had a dollar for every time Pearl applied more lipstick. "Didn't you just do that?"

"It never hurts to have fresh lipstick on. A girl's best friend is this little tube. Never leave home without it."

Rose Ellen could think of many things that she would consider important. Lipstick wasn't one of them.

The local Senior Society was always a cheerful sight. Sunshine usually streamed in through the many oversized windows. Behind the building was a beautifully landscaped patio area that offered a breathtaking view of the city.

The building was spacious and housed a library, activity rooms and a nice dance floor. You could play everything from card games to dominoes during the day, or take a painting class. The organization hosted line dancing and exercise groups and often brought in health care professions, who offered free blood pressure, cholesterol and glucose tests.

Saturday nights the place was abuzz with country dancers wearing western shirts, Stetsons and sporting Justin boots. It was a must for women to don sparkly jeans, lots of jewelry and accessorize their boots with rhinestone studded chains.

There were also special dances like Sock Hops, where attendees came dressed in poodle skirts and rolled up jeans. Root beer floats were served during the break, and the evening always ended with a 1950's doo-wop tune by the Spaniels.

Goodnight, Sweetheart, well it's time to go.
I hate to leave you, but I really must say
Oh, goodnight, Sweetheart, goodnight.

The Senior Senior Prom was always a big hit. It was fun to wear something a bit fancier and dance to the music of Tyler Junior College's famous Big Band. Usually, the oldest attendees were named king and queen of the prom.

By far, the most popular event held at the Senior Society was the weekly potluck. You didn't have to learn dance steps or card game rules. You just had to show up with something that was edible and be prepared to eat a lot.

The Senior Society's main room was packed as Rose Ellen and Pearl walked in with their respective dishes. Tables were already full of goodies like King Ranch Casserole, candied sweet potatoes, fried chicken, black eyed peas and homemade biscuits.

Most senior women still liked to show off their cooking skills and since many were widows, the supper was an opportune time to prepare and share a special dish, like avocado deviled eggs or Shoofly Pie.

Hot coffee, sweet tea and juicy gossip were also on the menu. But camaraderie was the most popular portion of the weekly potluck.

Rose Ellen tried to sneak her cookies onto the dessert table. The Brookshire Brothers bakery made wonderful cookies, but she still felt guilty, as she put them down between a buttermilk pie with made from scratch crust and a beautifully decorated, three-layer cake.

She turned around only to bump into Nelda, toting

her signature gigantic purse that looked more like a small suitcase.

"Well, what have we here? You didn't even bother to bake something?"

"Remember, I live in a tiny house. I don't have much of a kitchen."

Nelda sniffed, "You could have at least put them on a plate, rather than bringing them in that tacky, plastic box."

She had a point. Nobody would have a clue they weren't homemade, if Rose Ellen had brought them in piled up on one of her colorful Fiesta plates.

Nelda sashayed away. Pearl crossed her arms and gave Nelda's back a "go to hell" look.

"She is so hateful, bless her heart," Pearl said, adding the phrase that made even the most vicious insult acceptable.

Rose Ellen started to open her mouth and say something really mean, like the fact that Nelda was overweight. That wouldn't be right, Rose Ellen decided, since just about every older woman she knew was somewhat overweight.

Besides that, the top button on her own pants—the pair that fit perfectly last year--was literally digging into her skin. She discretely unbuttoned her top button and thought about how it was best not to light a match while holding the gasoline.

Damn hormones, she thought. It was too bad you couldn't bank your young, raging ones and save them for later to combat age-related issues like extra weight, wrinkles and upper lip hair—the kind of thick hair that used to be abundant on your head.

Rose Ellen also remembered her mother's advice:

"Make sure your words are sweet, in case you have to eat them later."

That motto was hard to live by when it came to dealing with a woman who spent a lifetime going after other women's men, particularly if you had an image of her kissing your boyfriend stuck in your head for half a century.

"There she goes again," Rose Ellen grumbled. "Look at her now. Better circle the wagons, boys. Here she comes."

Nelda was almost galloping across the floor toward a fresh widower. She had actually waited a respectable amount of time before approaching this one. It had been almost three weeks since the funeral.

Pearl disgustedly grunted. "Wait for it, Ex. Just wait."

Within seconds, Nelda was rubbing his arm and giving him her standard "I'm here if you need me" speech.

"Oh Pearl, the poor old thing looks like a deer caught in headlights. Nelda might as well throw a lasso around him. It would be less obvious."

Rose Ellen and Pearl began giggling when Ruth came up behind them, barbecued green bean casserole in hand.

"Let me put this down, so I can get my hugs," Ruth said.

She carefully shoved a few other dishes aside to make her specialty more noticeable on the already heavily laden table. A simple potluck in East Texas was always more like a feast for a couple of hundred hungry ranch hands.

It was a given that everyone was greeted with a

hug. Ruth claimed she did the loose, sideways hug so she wouldn't mess up her makeup. Pearl always thought it might have something to do with the fact that she thought her red hair dye might rub off on some cowboy's white, starched shirt, if she did the closer, frontal hug.

"Did you hear about the third Seventeen Dollar Murder?" Ruth asked.

"I know," Rose Ellen replied. "It's just awful. I can't imagine why anyone would do that. And why target senior women?"

"Boomer/seniors, honey. I think I prefer that label," Pearl corrected her.

Ruth rolled her eyes and Pearl ignored her. "They need to really concentrate on what else the women have in common."

"That's true," Ruth said. "There has to be some other connection."

The three began discussing the fact that the seventeen dollars in cash left at each of the crime scenes must be the key to the mysterious deaths.

News reports had also emphasized the idea that the slayings seemed like overkill. Stabbing and strangling the victims meant the murderer wanted to make sure each woman was good and dead.

But was it one murderer? That had not been proven, but it was likely since all three victims were about the same age and had been left clutching seventeen dollars. The second two homicides could have been a copycat killer, but who knew? There were still so many unanswered questions.

Rose Ellen was relieved when the lights flashed. That meant it was time for the blessing. Meals in the

South were generally not consumed until the diners prayed. At the Senior Society potluck, attendees assumed retired preacher Johnny Ray would lead the prayer, which was usually long-winded.

If it was time to pray, it meant that Pearl could not start in again about how they should assist the police investigating the unsolved homicides. As soon as the blessing was over, people would start swarming the tables, and Pearl, hopefully, would be more interested in filling her mouth with food than filling other people's heads with nonsense about boomer/senior sleuths.

A screeching noise suddenly resonated throughout the room. At first, it sounded like feedback from the loud speaker.

Everyone turned toward Johnny Ray, who had just begun to utter a few words to bless the food. He looked bewildered and tapped the top of his microphone.

The high-pitched shrieking sound continued, but it soon became obvious that it wasn't coming from the equipment. Its origin was near one of the long tables. Had someone's dish crashed on to the floor?

Pearl and Rose Ellen turned almost in unison to see Nelda and Ruth yelling at each other.

"You always do this!" shouted Nelda. "Don't try to hand me the recipe! Everybody knows how to make barbecued green bean casserole and yours is nothing special. Besides, you probably left the green beans off the recipe card."

"Well, I never! You are the one that left the chicken off your recipe for chicken casserole!" Ruth shouted back.

"At least my hair color is natural. I don't have to

get mine from a bottle!"

"No way!" screamed Ruth. "No woman in her seventies has naturally blonde hair, you hussy!"

"I'm still in my sixties!" Nelda exclaimed.

"Oh, right, Nelda. You've been in your late sixties for the past three years. You are such a liar. I ought to snatch you bald-headed!"

Before Nelda could reply, Ruth lunged toward her and tossed a blonde wig into the air. Nelda reached up and grabbed her head, let out an ear-piercing shriek, and shoved Ruth to the floor.

They became one frenzied ball as each grappled for control. Sensible shoes and words that older southern ladies did not usually utter in public were flying in all directions.

Mouths were dropping around the room like the wave in a football stadium, as the two evenly matched women continued to roll around like a Tom and a cat in heat. For a few minutes, everyone stood frozen and stunned.

Most of the potluck attendees had never witnessed a "girl" fight, let alone one between senior women. It was like watching a house burn down, awful and captivating at the same time.

Johnny Ray dropped his microphone and rushed toward the women. They pulled him down as he tried to break up the fight, and the three became a giant mass of flailing arms and legs.

Suddenly a panting Johnny Ray managed to raise his head and scream, "Stop! Stop! She's not moving!"

Johnny Ray rolled off to one side. Ruth's face was as red as her dyed hair, and she was straddling Nelda's chest.

"Somebody call 9-1-1!" Johnny Ray begged. "Oh, my God!" he shouted as he frantically dragged Ruth off a motionless Nelda.

She lay flat on her back. Johnny Ray reached out from his position on the floor and nudged her. Nelda remained perfectly still. He pulled himself up, nudged her more vigorously and then began to violently shake her limp body.

"Oh, please, Nelda, wake up!" he said as he gave her face a mild slap. There was no response at all.

Nearby, Ruth lay gasping for air. Johnny Ray had pushed her off Nelda into a very unladylike position. Normally, she wouldn't be caught dead with no shoes, torn pantyhose and her legs sprawled apart like a chicken on a chopping block.

Ruth seemed to be totally unaware of anything but catching her breath. She clutched her chest and made no attempt to find a more mannerly pose.

For a few minutes, the potluck attendees didn't react. Then cell phones began popping out of pockets and purses all over the room as Johnny Ray begged, "Please! We need help!"

He staggered to his feet and looked down at Ruth, who was still grasping her chest. He fumbled in his shirt pocket, nervously searching for his phone. It noisily crashed onto the linoleum floor as he shakily tried to retrieve it.

Johnny Ray stared at his smart phone in disbelief and wildly threw his hands in the air as he addressed Ruth.

"Look what you've done! I think Nelda's...," he nervously gasped. "Nelda's dead! Oh, dear God! Ruth, you've killed her!"

Three

Rose Ellen covered her mouth in horror. Was Nelda dead? What happened? Did she have a heart attack? Did Ruth cause that?

Everything seemed to move in slow motion. Johnny Ray stood with his hands on his head and mumbled, "She's dead... she's dead."

Ruth crumpled into a fetal position. A few people sat down beside Nelda, who was as stiff as a corpse at a viewing. One woman was rubbing her arms, and another was calling her name, with no response.

Somehow, Johnny Ray managed to retrieve his microphone and tried to warn the crowd to stay back. Horrified seniors began to stir as the sound of sirens drowned out his pleas.

Suddenly, the room became a flurry of EMTs rushing toward Nelda. It looked like they were injecting her with something, and a mask was placed on her ghostly, white face.

Rose Ellen felt a rush of guilt about the insults she and Pearl had been hurling at her nemesis. She detested Nelda, but she certainly didn't wish her dead.

Someone from the crowd announced, "She's moving!"

Johnny Ray immediately ran in front of the EMTs hovered over Nelda, frantically spread out his arms and shouted, "Stay back! Stay back!"

He paused, took a deep breath, and said, "Let us pray."

Johnny Ray tried to ask for Nelda's recovery, but most of the seniors were focused on the dramatic scene unfolding in front of them.

Pearl craned her neck to get a better view of Nelda and caught a glimpse of her being loaded onto the stretcher.

"She's moving her arm!"

"Praise the Lord!" Johnny Ray exclaimed, as he, too, saw Nelda's slight movement.

"I hope it isn't just a nerve or something," said Rose Ellen. "I've heard about things like that."

"Me, too," Pearl softly echoed.

Ruth had been placed in a chair and appeared to be all right. She tried to pull away from the medical personnel treating her.

She lunged forward and screamed, "I'm sorry, Nelda! I didn't mean to hurt you!" As the reality of the situation hit her, she burst into tears.

"I kinda feel sorry for her," Pearl said.

"I know what you mean. I don't think she ever intended to do any real harm to Nelda. She did snatch her bald-headed, though," Rose Ellen observed. "Hey look! You were right. Her arm is going up."

Nelda raised her right arm and gave a "thumbs up." It looked like she was trying to sit up on the gurney as they whisked her away to the ambulance.

Johnny Ray clapped one hand against his microphone as Nelda and her medical entourage left the Senior Society.

Hopefully, it wasn't anything too serious. Maybe Nelda would be okay. At least she wasn't dead and regaining consciousness was a good sign.

"I gave them my cell number," Johnny Ray

announced. "Somebody's gonna call us from the hospital as soon as they know anything about Nelda."

"I guess people are feeling optimistic, and none of this food is going to waste," said Rose Ellen.

The crowd that seemed motionless just minutes earlier went into action and pressed toward the food tables like a herd of cows following a hay truck.

"One thing about us. Even a crisis doesn't dull our taste buds," Pearl noted. "Especially for sweets. You'd think we wouldn't need a sugar rush after all the excitement."

It was true. Most seniors loved sugar, and the dessert table was the most popular at the potlucks. Diabetics weren't left out, either. The sugar free area featured pies, cakes and cookies made with artificial sweeteners.

"I wonder if it's because sweetness is one of our last tastes to wane, or maybe it's because indulging in sugary treats is one of the last vices we have left."

"I hear you," sighed Rose Ellen. "I still miss cigarettes, and I haven't smoked for over thirty years."

"I miss the hard stuff, but I just can't hold my liquor anymore--a glass of wine occasionally is usually all I can handle."

"Maybe that's a good thing, Pearl. Remember what too much alcohol did to us in our younger days? I recall praying to the porcelain goddess a time or two. Not something I want to do again."

Rose Ellen thought about the parties they attended at Tyler Junior College. Back then, they were considered wild when the main dish was Everclear and Grape Kool-Aid punch. They had never heard of fancy Jell-O shots or Beer Pong, and hardly anybody took drugs in their neck of the piney woods.

Years later, when Rose Ellen caught her teenage daughter with marijuana, Jennifer used the "Well, you did it" defense. But Ruth Ellen was quick to tell her that back in the sixties in East Texas, "the worst thing we did was get drunk and get pregnant."

As Rose Ellen and Pearl pushed their way toward the food tables, they saw a few men helping Ruth to her feet. She seemed a little wobbly, but okay.

"Hey, Ex. I wonder if Ruth has anything to do with the Seventeen Dollar Murders?"

"Don't be ridiculous! It was just a cat fight, plain and simple. The murders have you acting paranoid. You are starting to question everyone and everything."

"But she went after Nelda like a pit bull. I've never seen her act that way. Usually, she is pretty well mannered, and let me tell you—that was not ladylike."

There she goes again with the boomer/senior sleuth talk, thought Rose Ellen. Pearl was the one acting like a pit bull. She just wasn't going to let go of her notion that two boomers with no experience could help solve three homicides.

"You've been watching too many episodes of *Lieutenant Joe Kenda Homicide Hunter*, Pearl."

"Don't you just love him? He is amazing. Can you believe he solved over three hundred cases in his career?"

"I know, and he also has beautiful, blue eyes. I watch that Investigation Discovery show, too. But that doesn't make us Joe Kenda."

"Well," Pearl replied. "I have picked up some tips from his episodes about what to look for in murder cases."

Their conversation was interrupted by Johnny Ray. Perfect timing, thought Rose Ellen.

"I'm just so relieved that Nelda isn't dead, and Ruth felt well enough to eat a little something. We have a lot to be thankful for right now," he said.

Ruth was near the dessert table, wolfing down a giant slice of Mississippi Mud Pie. Rose Ellen rolled her eyes. "Nothing like a cat fight to make a girl hungry."

Johnny Ray blushed a little and quickly changed the subject. "Are you ladies coming to the Ben Wheeler Feral Hog Festival?"

That was another great thing about the Tyler, Texas, area. Not only were there activities aimed at seniors, there were lots of other free, fun festivals for everyone to enjoy.

The Feral Hog Festival in the quaint little town of Ben Wheeler was an annual event that featured a wild hog cook off and lots of vendors, selling everything from handmade jewelry, to pottery sculpted by local artists.

On top of the great food, there was "pickin on the porch" all day long. It was fun to listen to local musicians, like the Texas Express band. There was even a tiny, plywood dance floor for those who wanted to boot scoot.

"The festival is always fun, Johnny Ray," said Rose Ellen. Her mouth watered just thinking about all the free samples of great barbecue that would be available in Ben Wheeler, the town that touted itself as the "Wild Hog Capital of Texas."

Johnny Ray nodded. "I know I don't have to explain it to you people, but a lot of folks don't understand how much of a problem the hogs are for Texas and why we encourage thinning out their population."

"That's right," Rose Ellen replied. "I read in the paper just last week that there were over 2.6 million feral hogs in our state. They cause millions of dollars in damage ever year to crops, gardens and yards."

"They have very destructive feeding habits, so it's a continuous problem," Pearl added. "There have also been lots of fatal car wrecks, because it's hard to see those hogs at dusk when they dart across a dark, county road."

"After some of the hogs are killed, we do our part," Johnny Ray said with a grin. "Me and a few fellows from the church are in the cook off again. Come by and get a little taste of our wild hog meat. This year we have a different sauce. I think you are gonna like it, ladies."

Ben Wheeler was just a half hour drive from Tyler and was one of the many unique towns in Texas. Originally called Cough, it was named after mail carrier and Kentucky native, Benjamin F. Wheeler, in 1878.

Every time anyone mentioned the town's unusual name, Rose Ellen thought about the little yellowed newspaper clipping she had found in her mother's belongings after the funeral.

Combining unique Texas town names and their distances, the list humorously stated facts like, "From Dawn to Noonday, 500 miles; Noonday to Sunset, 160 Miles; Ding Dong to Bells, 200 miles; Eden to Paradise, 180 miles; Big Foot to Elbow, 270 miles; Telephone to Telegraph, 325 miles and Pep to Energy,

285 miles."

She smiled as she recalled her mother saying, "A lot of the little towns in Texas have 'Welcome' and 'Hurry Back' on the same sign."

Rose Ellen and Pearl assured Johnny Ray that they wouldn't miss the Ben Wheeler Feral Hog Festival. How could anybody resist tasting dozens of tantalizing barbecue dishes? It was worth risking possible heartburn, and that could be squelched with a handful of Tums.

"Can I sit with you, ladies?" Johnny Ray asked as they all looked around for seats that weren't taken.

Seniors were pretty territorial and most sat in the exact spot each time there was an event, like the potluck. There could be hell to pay if you dared to sit in a chair with an invisible "reserved" sign on it.

Rose Ellen and Pearl usually just looked for empty seats they knew were probably available. It was easy enough to ask if they were taken.

"Sure, Johnny Ray. You are always welcome to sit with us," Pearl replied. "Hey, Ex, there are three together over there."

They walked to a mostly empty table and dove in like everyone else. Nothing like a lot of wonderful food to quiet a room.

Rose Ellen looked around and noted the fact that things weren't much different at the Senior Society than they had been at the John Tyler High School cafeteria years before. The AARP crowd was just as divided.

There was the self-proclaimed Cool Kids' Table, which consisted of the old Tyler oil money and society crowd. The Bookworm Table was full of quiet, studious types, while the Drama Table included boomers who acted in high school and still dabbled in little theater productions.

The old jocks tended to sit together and talk about their glory days scoring touchdowns and tackling opponents. Former cheerleaders and drill team members often joined them.

There was a Singles Table, but it was mostly occupied by widows and widowers. Pearl wouldn't sit there because the women--who greatly outnumbered the men—fiercely competed for the few unsuspecting widowers.

"I want no part of that," she said. "I had a good one. I don't think I would be so lucky the next time, so I won't even take a chance. Plus, I don't have time to train a new one."

The Singles or Widows' Table was out as far as Rose Ellen was concerned, too. She wasn't a widow, and the last thing she wanted to do was try to converse with Nelda, who always sat there.

Rose Ellen figured she would probably throw up all over the table if she had to listen to the baby talk Nelda used when a naïve, available man was within her grasp.

Like Pearl had once remarked, "You can read Nelda like a book. Too bad you can't shut her up like one."

On top of their history, Nelda was more than irritating. Still, the thought that her nemesis almost met her maker made Rose Ellen twinge again with guilt.

Pearl liked to say that wherever the duo sat, it was the Good Times Table. They tried to avoid talk about politics and religion.

Jokes were abundant and could be a bit off color, unless Johnny Ray sat down. Even the Good Times Table folks respected a retired preacher enough to stick with clean jokes.

Unfortunately, the dumber jokes were often repeated, like the one that asked "In Texas, what do a tornado and a divorce have in common?... Somebody's gonna lose a trailer."

They dined on everything from chicken spaghetti, spicy bean dip and tamales, to creamed corn, meat loaf and fried okra.

Their dinner was interrupted by a call from the hospital. Johnny Ray relayed the good news to the crowd. Nelda had probably passed out from stress, but would be fine. "Thank you, Lord," he said, and the diners clapped in agreement.

"I'm as full as an East Texas tick," Rose Ellen said. "But I always save room for dessert. Besides that, we need to celebrate the good news about Nelda."

"Amen," echoed Pearl. "I got peach cobbler. My favorite! I'm never too full for that tasty treat."

They had gone to the dessert table first, before Peggy's peach cobbler disappeared. Nothing like a pastry dish made from peaches right off the tree. And Peggy's backyard was full of fruit trees. She usually froze the extra summer peaches, so she could use them all year long.

Johnny Ray's plate was stacked with brownies, and Rose Ellen had chosen chess pie, as well as Peggy's dessert. The three ate their sweets in silence, until they couldn't eat one more bite.

"What happened with Nelda makes you think, doesn't it?" Pearl asked as she finished the last morsel of peach cobbler.

"Oh, yes. But I think Nelda was ready, if it had been her time," said Johnny Ray. "She's a good Christian woman."

"I don't mean that. It makes me think about all the things I still want to do. You know, like a bucket list."

"Oh," Johnny Ray commented, like he had never considered making a bucket list. "So, what is it you want to do before you die?"

"I have always wanted to dance on a table. I mean, I may have done that back in my Tyler Junior College Days. If I did, it was probably at one of our parties. So, alcohol was involved and I don't remember. But I would like to dance on a table and actually remember it."

Johnny Ray looked at Pearl as if she had smacked him upside the head. Rose Ellen tried not to laugh, but a little giggle came out anyway.

Apparently, Johnny Ray was thinking more in terms of overseas missionary work, volunteering after a natural disaster, serving at a soup kitchen or some other equally honorable endeavor.

He didn't know much about Pearl, thought Rose Ellen. If he did, he would have just taken her comments in stride.

"We...Well..." he stuttered. "I guess that would be okay. I mean, if it was done in good taste."

"Oh, I wouldn't do anything that would be scandalous. If I can—I just want to jump up on a table and rock out to something like Donna Summer's *Hot Stuff.*"

Johnny Ray began choking. Pearl slapped him on the back several times and then raised his left arm.

"Are you all right?"

"Yes," he gasped. "Must have been something I ate."

Sure, thought Rose Ellen. Something you ate. Don't think so. Off color jokes might be taboo, but telling a former preacher you want to dance on a table to *Hot Stuff* was not off limits to Pearl. Johnny Ray would probably think twice before he sat at the Good Times Table again.

He took a few raspy breaths. "I'm okay, now."

Pearl lowered his left arm. "I thought for a minute there I was going to have to do the Heimlich Maneuver on you."

Johnny Ray breathed a big sigh of relief. At least she didn't say anything about mouth to mouth resuscitation.

Pearl was bold, feisty, a bit flirty and loved to push the envelope too far. But she was no Nelda, thought Rose Ellen. That woman would have planted her Pink Parfait lips on a gasping Johnny Ray in a New York minute. Nelda wouldn't just push the envelope until it fell off the table—she would scoot it all the way across the room.

The crowd was thinning, and people were retrieving their plates and dishes. Most were marked with masking tape labels and names printed in big, bold letters. That way, no one would walk off with someone else's empty plate or leftovers.

There usually weren't many leftovers and if there were, they seemed to be the few healthy dishes. Homemade casseroles and desserts like pecan pie and Better than Sex Cake disappeared instantly.

Rose Ellen scanned the area to see if anyone was

looking. Her plastic box still had a half dozen cookies left in it. How embarrassing, she thought.

Next time, she would make more of an effort to bake something, or at least use her own plate, instead of a store container. There was almost nothing worse than leaving a southern potluck with a dish that hadn't been licked clean.

She considered hiding the left-over cookies in her purse, but then the crumbs would make a real mess. Rose Ellen wrapped her arm around the plastic carton and hurried toward the exit.

"Ex, wait for me!" Pearl called as she tried to catch up.

"See you at the Feral Hog Festival, Johnny Ray!" Rose Ellen shouted as she scurried out the door.

Four

On top of offering a lot for baby boomers and older seniors, and hosting festive events, the Tyler area was a beautiful place to live, particularly in the spring and fall.

Autumn had come early to East Texas, and that meant the countryside was dotted with multi-colored trees. Pines weren't the only trees native to the area. Oaks, elms, pecans and sweetgums were among the many varieties that filled the rolling hills.

The country lane that wound its way to Ben Wheeler was framed by a palette of purple, yellow and dark orange hues. A cool breeze gently carried a few crisp leaves to the ground, and the sky was blue and cloudless.

Rose Ellen and Pearl arrived at the Feral Hog Festival with Kenny in tow. Even Pearl agreed that they couldn't turn down his request to come with them. That wouldn't have been mannerly. Besides that, maybe it meant that he was finally ready to jump start his life without Bess.

The strains of *Five Pound Bass* floated through the air from the Pickin Porch Pavilion as the trio pulled into the parking area.

"I love the way they do Robert Earl Keen's song. Texas Express is a great band!" Pearl exclaimed.

Texas Express was a foursome that included mature men who often played for local dances, like the ones at the Senior Society. They were popular, experienced musicians, and their extensive repertoire included everything from rock and roll and rhythm and blues, to western swing and traditional country songs.

"I like to hear that guy with the gray hair sing," Pearl added. "He is so cute."

"Pearl, they all have gray hair. That is, if they have any hair left," Rose Ellen sighed.

"Very true, Ex. But sometimes you can't tell whether a man's hair is graying or gone, because most older men around these parts wear cowboy hats. Hey, this is a polka. Come on Kenny, let's cut a rug!"

With that, Pearl tried to grab Kenny and spin him around in the grassy parking field. He quickly stepped behind Rose Ellen.

"I don't dance. Well, I did maybe once-- with Bess."

"Now Kenny, remember that Asleep at the Wheel song? It says you gotta *Dance with Who Brung You, Swing with Who Swung You.*"

"No I don't!"

"Pearl, I don't think he wants to dance."

"Well, okay, Kenny. I won't make you dance with me this time. You know, you're as skittish as a new foal."

"It's not that. I just don't dance --at all." He stayed behind Rose Ellen as they made their way to the Pickin Porch Pavilion.

Tantalizing whiffs of barbecue wafted through the air as the band finished the last verse of *Five Pound Bass.*

What a great, lively song, thought Rose Ellen. No wonder Pearl wanted to dance. That version would make anybody want to get up and polka—except

"Oh, that makes sense," Pearl said. "Like my mother used to tell me about gifts from my grandmother. If she gave us something we didn't really like, or we thought was too childish or tacky, we weren't supposed to say anything but 'thank you'."

"How about bigger than Dallas?" asked Kenny. "That one seems pretty obvious."

"I think it has two meanings," Rose Ellen explained. "Besides meaning something that is really big, it can also refer to something right in front of you."

Pearl interrupted. "Like, when you can't find your keys, and then you see them bigger than Dallas right in front of you on the kitchen counter?"

"Yep. I know we have all done that a time or two." Rose Ellen laughed. Kenny smiled and nodded his head. Forgetfulness was part of aging. Thank goodness, the three of them seemed to have normal memory loss and not dementia.

"Hey, the band is back. I'm gonna request a tune," Pearl announced.

She headed toward the bandstand. Rose Ellen wondered if it was just an excuse to get close to the player Pearl had referred to as cute.

The lead singer shook his head. "He says they don't know the *Dill Pickle Rag*," Pearl reported as she approached the table. "But they will be happy to play my other request, *Folsom Prison Blues*."

"I don't care if they do play Johnny Cash. I'm not dancing," Kenny retorted.

Maybe Pearl's prodding was helping Kenny develop a backbone, thought Rose Ellen. The more she pushed, the more assertive he seemed to become.

"Fine. I can dance by myself." Pearl hopped up on the plywood dance floor and started spinning around like a go-go girl to the Johnny Cash tune. All she needed was a pair of white boots and matching fish net stockings.

Rose Ellen envied Pearl's spunk. She didn't seem to care what anyone thought. She just had fun, even though occasionally, when she pushed the envelope too far, it fell off the table.

That was also one of the few advantages of getting older. You could shed the idea that what other people thought mattered.

There were limits to that, but Pearl never did anything that was harmful or would hurt someone's feelings. Well, except when it came to Nelda. A woman who pushed the envelope off the table and then clean across the room deserved whatever she got.

Rose Ellen also envied the fact that Pearl lived for the moment. It wasn't because she was getting older. Pearl had always been that way and often chided Rose Ellen.

"You wanna know how the dance ends before you take one step," Pearl had said. "Life doesn't work that way. Just jump in, hang on, follow the beat and see what happens."

Maybe that was one reason Pearl didn't like to be late. Being late meant she might miss a precious minute of fun.

"Have you thought about what you are going to wear to the Monster Bash at the Senior Society?" Pearl asked, panting a bit. She was a little short of breath from her performance.

The annual Halloween party was coming up. The

place would be decorated with pumpkins, fake cobwebs and spiders. Treats often included orange iced cupcakes, black jelly beans and Peggy's cookies that looked like severed digits.

Her finger shaped cookies included almond sliver fingernails and jagged edges smeared with red jam. The gruesome dessert also featured a fake cleaver stuck in the middle of the plate. Despite initial groans, the delicious Severed Finger Cookies usually disappeared quickly.

It was always fun to come up with a costume, and some people were particularly creative. One year, a couple sported Army fatigues. He wore the bottoms and a sign around his neck that read, "Lower G.I." She wore the top and her sign said, "Upper G.I."

"I don't know, Pearl. I can't wear my pioneer girl outfit again this year. I've gotta come up with something, though. What about you?"

"I thought about making a flowered headband and a wearing a skirt with one of Mom's old flour sack aprons. You know, something that would look like a German fraulein."

"That would be cute! And fun, if you did the polka!"

"If anybody would dance the polka with me." Pearl shot Kenny a dirty look. He folded his arms and glared back at her.

"I also thought about running up to Lindale, where Miranda Lambert's store is. The Pink Pistol has some really cute cowgirl things, like hot pink boots, little blingy skirts and holsters that match."

Rose Ellen pictured Pearl as a bright pink cowgirl in a skirt made for twenty-five-year-old legs. That would definitely qualify as an envelope pushed off the table. She rubbed her stomach and wondered if she had any Pepto-Bismol in her purse.

"What about you, Kenny? Are you going?"

"I don't know. Bess was the creative sort. I'm not. I don't think I could come up with a costume, and I don't really like to get out much."

Rose Ellen was well aware of that. She reminded herself about encouraging him to get out more and make new friends, so he would stop leaning on her all the time.

"Come on. You're having fun today, aren't you? It would be easy to do something like a ghost costume. All you need is an old, white sheet. You could just cut some holes in it for your eyes."

"Would you help me?"

"Sure, Kenny," Rose Ellen answered. It was the last thing she wanted to do. But if she helped him create a costume, it would force him to attend the Monster Bash. Then, he might meet other people that he could hang out with.

"What would I bring for snack time?"

Oh, good grief, thought Rose Ellen. Snack time? He sounded like a kindergartner. She wondered if Bess had done everything for Kenny, including telling him when to go to the bathroom and to be sure and wash his hands.

She bit her tongue. "Just do like I do. Run by Brookshire Brothers and grab something. You know, at Halloween they always have those cookies with orange sprinkles and purple icing on them."

"Oh. I guess I could do that."

Rose Ellen just hoped that Kenny didn't want her

to tag along with him to the grocery store. Surely, he could manage to find brightly colored Halloween cookies in the bakery department.

"I heard they are gonna have a smoke machine and everything. Maybe Texas Express will be playing," Pearl said.

"I still won't dance."

"You don't have to," Rose Ellen assured him. "Some people can't dance or don't want to, so they just listen to the music and socialize."

"And eat the goodies," Pearl added, ignoring Kenny's last remark about dancing. "I like those popcorn balls Ruth brings. I wonder if she puts a touch of vinegar in them. They don't seem to stick to your teeth like some popcorn balls do. And that's real helpful when the teeth aren't yours."

"Okay. I guess I can go. Can we ride together?"

"That would be fine, Kenny. I will just plan to pick you up. Speaking of being picked up, I wonder if any charges were filed against our two senior cage fighters?"

Pearl laughed and said, "I doubt it. They probably talked to some of the folks that went on to the hospital behind the ambulance and found out it was just a cat fight. Nelda and Ruth were both at fault. Hey…What in the Sam Hill? What is that noise?"

Pop! Pop! Pop! Sharp sounds resonated loudly throughout the festival.

Rose Ellen jumped to her feet, followed by Kenny and Pearl.

"Oh, my God!" shouted Pearl. "That sounds like gunshots!"

Suddenly, there was another round of popping

sounds. People began screaming and running in all directions. Band members dropped their instruments and fled from the Pickin Porch Pavilion.

"What's happening?" Kenny frantically asked.

"Hell, I don't know!" Pearl blurted out.

"Get down!" ordered Rose Ellen. The three dove under the picnic table where they had been sitting and hovered together.

"Let's get out of here!" Kenny demanded.

"No! We don't know where the shots are coming from. We might be sitting ducks here, but at least we have some cover. If somebody is shooting and we run, then they can easily pick us off. Pearl, can you tell which direction the shots are coming from?"

"No. Well, maybe from behind Moore's Country Store. I'm not sure."

Pop! Pop! Pop! The trio cringed in unison as they heard another round of ear piercing tones.

What was happening? Was it the Seventeen Dollar Murderer? Surely not, thought Rose Ellen. Most killers don't change their M.O., and the three recent homicide victims were stabbed and strangled, not shot.

But who was shooting up the Ben Wheeler Feral Hog Festival and why? Rose Ellen's mind was racing.

She tried to put the recent, gruesome murders out of her head. She had to try to figure out what to do next. But what could they do?

"Mama!" A small child was standing near their table and crying. Somehow in the confusion, she ended up alone.

Pearl immediately crawled out from under the table and grabbed the little girl. Instantly, she shoved the child between them.

"It's okay, honey. We'll find your mama soon," Pearl whispered, holding the tot near her.

Rose Ellen looked down at Pearl. "You're bleeding! You tore your pants on that gravel over there, and look at your knee. You really scraped it."

Pearl didn't seem to hear a word that Rose Ellen said. She gently rocked the frightened girl and repeated, "It's okay, honey."

What a good heart, thought Rose Ellen. Pearl had her idiosyncrasies, but no one could dispute the fact that she was a brave, caring soul who was totally selfless when confronted by a life-threatening situation.

"I don't hear anything," Kenny said. "Did they stop shooting?"

"I don't know," Rose Ellen responded as questions bombarded her brain. Had the shooting ended? Why had it started in the first place? Was just one person firing a gun?

What was the world coming to if you couldn't even go to a local festival without being targeted? What was going on? Was it the Seventeen Dollar Murderer? Had he changed his M.O.? Was the shooter even a man?

Five

The sharp, popping sounds had subsided, or at least it seemed that way. People were scattered everywhere around the feral hog festival grounds. Some lay flat on the grass, while others crouched under picnic tables, like Rose Ellen, Pearl and Kenny.

A grateful mother spotted Pearl with her daughter and embraced them both. She had been horrified to discover that she and her child had become separated during all the confusion.

Two police cars roared up, followed by a Van Zandt County Sheriff's vehicle. An officer jumped from the car and raced to the stage.

"It's all right, everybody! No one is shooting, so if anyone is carrying a weapon, please be advised. This is not a shooting! Put any weapons you might have away. We have the situation under control," the officer announced.

What happened? If it wasn't a shooting, what was it? The deputy quickly explained that the popping noises were made by teenagers setting off illegal fireworks behind Moore's Country Store.

Fireworks were only allowed during certain time periods, like around the Fourth of July and New Year's, and personal use was not permitted inside most Texas city borders.

The deputy continued, "As you all know, on top of the other laws, it is illegal to buy fireworks if you are under sixteen. We are confident that it was just these three boys, and they have been taken into custody. We will explore all possible violations and appropriate punishment will be administered."

"That's a relief," sighed Kenny.

Rose Ellen started to respond with a comment about the stupidity of shooting off fireworks illegally in a community that was already edgy because of three homicides.

She was interrupted by her Beatles' ringtone. "Yes, we are okay. I know, honey. It is all right. I will call you when I get home."

"That had to be Jennifer," Pearl stated.

"Yep. Can you believe a bunch of people already tweeted about this? Here we are possibly under siege, and some people think what they need to do is pull out their smart phones and go to a social media site. My daughter said it is on Facebook, too!"

It was horrible enough that facts about The Seventeen Dollar Murders made the national news. Then, a video of Nelda and Ruth's cat fight had gone viral. And now, the area would once again be in the spotlight for the fireworks incident. None were representative of their normally tranquil, southern home--particularly the shocking slayings.

"All this social media stuff sometimes gets ridiculous. I'm glad I have a dumb phone. See," Pearl said as she pulled out her flip phone. "I know smart phones come in handy, but I can't see spending all my time posting stuff. I mean, who cares what I had for breakfast?"

"And that FaceTime thing and Skype...I know they are good for keeping up with the grandkids, but for some of these young people, that is their entire social life," Rose Ellen added.

"I'm not on any of those sites, and I don't have apps. I don't even answer my phone, unless I can see who's calling," Kenny stated. "There are too many telemarketers and scams these days. A lot of them are aimed at seniors, too."

"You got that right. Boy, I could use a drink right now. My heart is still pounding," said Pearl. "I could go for some of that Spike stuff," she continued, referring to the vodka made in San Antonio from cacti.

She patted her knee with a tissue and pulled a band-aid from her purse. "Almost as good as new," Pearl announced, applying the bandage. "I think I will settle for a frosty root beer and a homemade funnel cake."

Folks began emerging from their hiding places and several headed to the parking lot as Texas Express took the stage again.

"We're not gonna let a few dumb kids spoil today's fun, are we?" the lead singer asked. "Here's a good one to dance to!"

He began to belt out *I Won't Go Huntin' With Ya Jake (But I'll Go Chasin' Wimmin)*. There was nothing like a funny, old tune to get the crowd back into a festive mood.

"I guess you definitely won't dance to this one, will you Kenny?"

He shot Pearl another dirty look. Rose Ellen hated to admit it, but it was fun to watch Pearl mess with Kenny. At least it made him act like he was alive again.

Pearl headed to the nearest funnel cake vendor. Rose Ellen stayed with Kenny and as they sat in silence, her mind drifted back to the events that had recently taken place.

There had been a lot of excitement with the fight between Nelda and Ruth and then the fireworks escapade. Normally, the wildest thing in Tyler, Texas, was a baseball size hailstorm.

But three unsolved murders? Not only was that unusual in the piney woods, it was unheard of. Rose Ellen felt like dealing with the most vicious East Texas hailstorm would be better than worrying about who the next murder victim might be—or if there even would be another murder. Maybe they would catch the perpetrator soon, and the Seventeen Dollar Murders would be solved.

It would drive her crazy, she thought, if she didn't stop thinking about the horrific crimes. Rose Ellen closed her eyes and concentrated on the humorous Stuart Hamblen lyrics as Texas Express sang the last verse of *I Won't Go Huntin' With Ya Jake.*

Now I was headed for the general store when a silly thing I seen.

They make 'em in the city; it's called a magazine.

I turned to page thirty-two and look at what I found

Them gals wear clothes we ain't seen beneath them gingham gowns.

"That's disgusting," Kenny mumbled. The comment took Rose Ellen by surprise.

"What? It's just a silly song. You're not getting all politically correct on me now, are you, Kenny?"

"They are talking about floozies. They just flaunt themselves to entice a man. I don't like loose women."

"What? How did you get that out of a song about a

guy who wants to chase women? It's just for laughs."
Boy, thought Rose Ellen, Pearl's constant teasing
might be too much, after all. Kenny's negative attitude
seemed to be escalating.

"Most women are out to lure a man and then when
they get tired of him, they trick another one."

"Kenny, that's a bit extreme, don't you think? You
could say the same thing about some men. I think it's a
funny spoof. I wouldn't get offended if I heard a tune
about women chasing good looking men."

"Why did you get divorced?" Kenny suddenly
blurted out, ignoring Rose Ellen's point. His tone
seemed almost angry.

"Well, it certainly wasn't because I am a loose
woman. It was pretty much like a lot of couples. Over
the years, we grew apart. We don't hate each other or
anything. We just looked across the breakfast table one
morning and realized we didn't even know one another
anymore."

"I stuck with the first woman I ever kissed, and I
never even looked at anyone else."

"I guess I wasn't as loyal as you, Kenny. I never
cheated on my husband, but I wasn't going to live in a
relationship that had died, either."

Rose Ellen was baffled by Kenny's behavior. He
was coming out of his shell, but not in a good way.

"How long were you married?"

"Well, not that it is any of your business, Kenny,
but the answer is thirty-four years."

Kenny looked stunned. "Ah...oh," he stammered,
"that's how long Bess and I were married."

Rose Ellen felt guilty for lashing out at Kenny,
even though he deserved it. "I'm sorry. I know it's

been hard, and there's an empty place in your heart, now."

He lowered his head. "Yes, there is."

Maybe Kenny's attitude was based on some resentment, thought Rose Ellen. Could it be that he felt abandoned when he lost Bess?

Sometimes grief over the death of a loved one would rear its ugly head by turning the survivor into a person who blamed the spouse for dying. That resentment bred negativity and could create a personality that found fault with everything—even the lyrics to a humorous, country song.

"Kenny, you know Bess would want you to move forward in a positive way and be happy again."

"I know you are right. I'm sorry, too. I didn't mean to be so harsh. I'll try to be better."

"Want some funnel cake?" Pearl asked as she approached the picnic table. She held out three forks and a magnificent combination of deep fried dough covered with powdered sugar.

Good timing, thought Rose Ellen. She could use the interruption to change the subject. "Oh, yum. I'll take some of that."

"Thanks, me too," Kenny said, as he reached for a plastic fork.

As the trio munched on the sweet treat, Rose Ellen focused on the beautiful day. Despite the scare, it was a good day to be alive. Or maybe it was best to think that it was good to be alive because it was just a scare.

Pearl had voiced her opinion about living life to the fullest right after Nelda's apparent brush with death. Rose Ellen felt the same way about the potentially life-threatening event they had just witnessed.

Life was precious and each minute was a gift. Maybe she needed to think about making a bucket list, herself.

"Oh, look, that cute guy is gonna talk," said Pearl, pointing to the bandstand. "I just love his cowboy hat."

"Are we having a good time?" he shouted. "Put your hands together, and let's welcome this year's head of the Ben Wheeler Feral Hog Festival, Mr. Sonny Williams!"

A slender man in a white shirt and starched Levi's, topped with a large, shiny belt buckle stepped to the microphone. "Time to announce the winners of the contests."

He started by naming the top prizes in the best bean and wild hog chili contests. Rose Ellen and Pearl crossed their fingers in unison as the announcement was made for the Best Wild Hog Meat Contest.

"And the winner is...The First Baptist Church!"

Johnny Ray and his team members hurriedly made their way to the stage. He anxiously took the microphone. "Thank you. Thank you so much. This is exciting! It was a team effort, let me tell you. And our prize money will go to help with the good work we do at the First Baptist Church."

"Amen! Way to go, Johnny Ray!" Pearl shouted. "Let's go congratulate him."

The three made their way to the stage and met Johnny Ray as he came down the wooden steps.

"We're so proud!" Rose Ellen exclaimed.

"Congratulations," Kenny said, as he shook Johnny Ray's hand. "Good job."

Things were looking up, thought Rose Ellen.

Johnny Ray deserved an award after what he had been through with Nelda and Ruth at the Senior Society.

It almost seemed like their little neck of the piney woods was normal again. The sun was shining brightly in the beautiful, blue sky, and fall was in the air. They had enjoyed great food and good company at one of best annual festivals in East Texas. Well, the company was good when Kenny wasn't whiney or mean-spirited.

Maybe the Feral Hog Festival was the beginning of Kenny's road to recovery. He might have slipped a bit with his negative over reaction to the humorous words of *I Won't Go Huntin' With Ya Jake,* but at least he had made the effort to get out of the house. For him, that was a big step forward.

The entire day, so far, had passed without Pearl mentioning the fact that they should become boomer/senior sleuths and solve the Seventeen Dollar Murders.

They spent the next hour visiting the various vendors. Pearl picked up some feral hog soap for her nephew, who liked to hunt. Rose Ellen bought a bracelet made from pieces of polished brass and mother-of-pearl.

The potter was interesting to watch, as she molded a shapeless piece of clay into a slender vase. Finished products were on display, and Rose Ellen added a small bowl to her bracelet purchase. Her tiny house had room for that, and it was just too pretty to pass up.

Kenny was fascinated with the handmade knives featured at one venue. He listened intently as the craftsman carefully explained how he fashioned the handle of one.

Was the small, shrinking violet Kenny slowly blossoming into a bouquet of brightly colored Texas wildflowers? Rose Ellen was glad to see him finally interested in something other than his dead wife. Hopefully, he wouldn't revisit his negativity.

"Are y'all ready to go?"

Kenny and Pearl nodded their heads.

"Hey, Ex. I've got a great idea!"

"What's that?"

"Well, there's still some daylight left, and Nelly's Party Factory will be open until eight. You want to swing by there when we get back to Tyler and see what kind of costumes they might have?"

"Sure," Rose Ellen replied.

"I don't know," said Kenny. "I should be getting home."

The little shrinking violet was trying to overshadow the wildflowers. Time for action, thought Rose Ellen.

"Oh, come on, Kenny. It would be fun. We could see what they have and if we are all together, we won't duplicate our costumes."

"I hadn't thought of that. I guess it would be okay to go to Nelly's. But I haven't decided for sure if I am going to the Monster Bash."

"You told us you would!" Pearl reminded him. "You're going with us, and that means you have to wear a costume. Halloween will be here before you know it, so this is a perfect opportunity to get our outfits. We can help each other."

"Pearl's right," echoed Rose Ellen. "We can't walk into the Senior Society without costumes. We would practically be the only ones. You know everybody gets into the spirit and dresses up."

"But what about the sheet to make me a ghost costume, like we talked about?" asked Kenny. "Wouldn't that be okay?"

"That's still a possibility. But we might find something more original than that at the party store. You can't imagine how many different Halloween costumes they have. It's amazing."

"You are right about that, Ex. They have the traditional ones like monsters and story book characters. They also carry trendy costumes like current politicians and people that are in the news. They even have reality star costumes, like Kim Kardashian from *Keeping Up with the Kardashians.*"

Kenny winced, probably from a picture in his head of Pearl dressed in a costume made for someone as young and voluptuous as Kim Kardashian. "I think I will look at the more traditional costumes."

"Nothing wrong with that, Kenny. We will just see what suits us," Pearl replied.

Rose Ellen did her best to give Kenny a reassuring look when she saw the fear in his eyes. He was probably terrified that Pearl would try to insist that they go as giant bottles of mustard and ketchup. Or even worse--Raggedy Ann and Andy.

She had a thing about dragging people into her escapades, and Pearl got a kick out of being able to manipulate others to follow her lead.

Kenny was on the edge of coming out of the dark tunnel of grief. Rose Ellen made a silent vow. She would do her best to make sure he wasn't pushed too hard, as he inched his way into the "new normal." The last thing she needed was Kenny continuing to invite himself to her tiny house to watch old reruns of *Hee Haw* on RFD-TV.

"How much will a costume cost me?" Kenny inquired.

Rose Ellen resisted criticizing him for being cheap. Most everybody in their crowd was retired and faced the same financial issues. Budgets were tight, since Social Security for most folks was just enough to live on. Few of their friends had anything more than a meager pension or retirement plan.

Fixed incomes were normal, but most retirees could afford Halloween costumes, even if it meant cutting somewhere else. A lot of seniors felt they were finally entitled to spend more money on themselves, particularly for entertainment.

After pinching pennies to raise families, many boomers felt it was time to let go of some of what they had so carefully saved for years. You couldn't take it with you, your kids didn't earn it, and they would probably just blow inheritance money, anyway. So why not spend a few bucks on yourself while you could still enjoy it?

"Hey Ex, isn't there a three-hundred-dollar prize for first place in the Monster Bash Costume Contest?" Pearl asked.

"Yes, that's right. The Almost Heaven Assisted Living Center has donated the money. If we got first place, that would be one hundred dollars for each of us."

"Really?" Kenny's eyes lit up. "But if we didn't win, we would be out the cost of the costumes."

An image of Kenny's sock feet propped up on her little coffee table popped into Rose Ellen's mind.

"Well, you would still have fun; a costume isn't expensive and you could use it again, sometime."

Kenny let out a sigh. "I guess that's true. Maybe we could just see what they have."

They pulled into the parking lot, entered Nelly's Party Factory, and began to browse the colorful, crowded aisles. Rose Ellen wondered how they would ever pick costumes from the overwhelming selections.

Suddenly, Pearl stopped in the middle of an aisle featuring traditional costumes. "This is it!" she shrieked. "A terrific trio, y'all. We'd be crushing it in these matching outfits!" She pointed to a large display featuring *The Three Musketeers*.

"Oh boy," Kenny gulped. And then he started to sweat.

Six

Rose Ellen had to admit that the Alexander Dumas character costumes were impressive. The outfits included large plumed hats, long curly wigs, knicker type pants and shirts featuring bright blue, attached capes.

"Wow!" Pearl exclaimed. "All we need are those plastic swords from the Dollar Bin, like I bought for my grandsons. We could just put a belt or sash around our waists and stick the swords in them."

"I don't know," Kenny mumbled. "Aren't these costumes kind of flashy?"

"They are half price," Rose Ellen replied.

Kenny squinted and inspected a price tag. "I guess *The Three Musketeers* aren't as popular these days as stuff like *The Walking Dead*."

"You have boots and gloves, don't you Kenny?"

"Yes, I guess I have some that would work."

"There you go," Pearl declared, as she picked up three fake moustaches. "We could get these and we would be all set, wouldn't we?"

"Well..." Before Kenny could continue his sentence, Pearl headed for the checkout with an armload of costumes.

"It would be great fun and such a hoot," Rose Ellen said. "Don't you know people at the Senior Society would get a kick out of the three of us in our curly wigs and moustaches? And our group knows exactly who *The Three Musketeers* are."

Kenny reluctantly followed them to the checkout. He probably wasn't totally convinced, thought Rose Ellen, but it looked like he would go along with the idea. Maybe this was another little step on Kenny's road to recovery.

They loaded their costumes into the car and headed home. Kenny fell asleep in the back seat before they were half way there.

Pearl yawned in the passenger seat. "It has been quite a day, hasn't it?"

"Yes, it has. Fun, but there were some scary moments. I am so proud of you for facing danger like you did and pulling that little girl to safety."

"Don't give me too much credit, Ex. I didn't even think about it. I just reacted like any mother would."

Rose Ellen didn't believe that. Pearl had risked her life for a stranger, and that was truly special.

"It sure makes you think, doesn't it, Ex? I mean it could have been the Seventeen Dollar Murderer who was doing the shooting."

There she goes again with the boomer/senior sleuth stuff, Rose Ellen thought. But she was too tired to stop Pearl from carrying on about how two little old ladies could solve crimes that may have been committed by a serial killer.

"I keep thinking about what the women had in common—I mean other than the fact that they all lived around here, and they were all about the same age. I wonder what else they shared?"

Pearl was right. There had to be a reason senior women born during the post war baby boom years had been targeted. Did they know each other? Was it just a coincidence that all three bodies were dumped in areas where no one was around?

"I am just thinking aloud here," she said. "These crimes might be the work of two killers. Like maybe a man and a woman, or two men. You could interrogate one and get him to turn on the other one. You know, like Detective Garry McFadden does on that *I am Homicide* show."

Rose Ellen and Pearl were fans of that Investigation Discovery series, too, in addition to *Lieutenant Joe Kenda Homicide Hunter*. Many murders were solved on those true crime shows when one criminal cracked and turned on an accomplice.

"I love what Detective McFadden said on that one episode. Like if one bad guy throws the other under the bus, he'd be more than happy to drive the bus and run over both," Rose Ellen said with a laugh.

How would anyone—including the police, find even one suspect, let alone two? There was literally no physical evidence of any significance left behind. The killer or killers had been skillful at covering up three horrible crimes.

Rose Ellen felt herself doing exactly what she swore she wouldn't do—letting Pearl draw her into obsessing over the murders. She had to admit that the Seventeen Dollar Murders were intriguing. Still—a couple of mature, southern women could not solve homicides that had the local police buffaloed.

They rode in silence for a while. Kenny was still sleeping in the back seat, and Pearl looked like she was going to nod off, too.

"I wonder if anyone has googled them or checked their Facebook pages?" Pearl was apparently not interested in taking a nap, despite her fatigue.

"What made you think of that?"

"I don't know. I just wondered. That way you could see what else they might have in common."

"Surely, the cops have checked social media sites. That's standard today with crimes of this magnitude."

"I guess you are right, Ex. But I think I might just try that out of curiosity. It would be interesting to see if the three women had some of the same Facebook friends. I could also see if there were any posts or tweets about seventeen dollars."

"I feel like that has already been done, Pearl."

As Rose Ellen said the words, she wondered. Would the local police department have time to dig that deeply into all the possible social media sites the three victims might have participated in? Law enforcement staffs were stretched to the limit just about everywhere, and that included Tyler.

Before she had time to think about it, Rose Ellen blurted out, "You know, it wouldn't hurt if we did some checking like that, would it?"

"I thought you weren't interested in exploring my theories about the Seventeen Dollar Murders?"

"Well, you have some really good ideas and being retired, we have time to do some sleuthing."

"I knew you'd come around!" Pearl's voice was downright joyful. "Boomer/senior sleuths. That's us!"

A startled Kenny suddenly woke up. "What's wrong?"

"Nothing. We were just discussing the recent DRTs. You know, that stands for Dead Right There, because those women were deceased when they found them," Pearl replied, trying to sound like a detective on one of their favorite shows.

"Oh," Kenny sleepily mumbled. "What did you decide?"

"We were just speculating on how we might help the cops catch the perpetrator or perpetrators," Pearl continued.

"I think it was a woman."

"Why would you say that, Kenny?"

"Because women are mean."

There he goes again with the bitterness, thought Rose Ellen. She made a mental note to suggest grief counseling sometime soon. He was making a little progress, but it would probably take professional help for Kenny to stop blaming women for everything bad in the world, just because Bess had up and died on him.

She let out a disgusted sigh, and Kenny quickly added, "I know. I'm sorry. I told you I would try, but without Bess...I just don't know. It's so hard to look on the bright side."

Rose Ellen tried to ignore Kenny's comments. "I wonder if it is someone hiding in plain sight. You know, that's the case a lot of times on those real-life murder mystery shows."

"You are right, Ex. But I just can't picture anyone in our crowd as the Seventeen Dollar Murderer."

"True. People who commit violent crimes aren't usually older folks. Statistics prove that."

Before Kenny could make any more negative remarks about women, Rose Ellen turned onto the road where she and Kenny lived.

"Aren't you going to take Pearl home?"

"No, Kenny. We have some girl things to do." Rose Ellen was proud of herself for the quick response.

She didn't want him inviting himself to hang around. It had been a long day. Besides, it might be interesting to surf the net to see if they could uncover more information about the three murdered women.

That wouldn't really be considered sleuthing, she told herself. She and Pearl were not qualified to work murder cases by any stretch of the imagination. But what would it hurt to noodle around on the internet and see what they could find?

Kenny reluctantly got out of the car, his bags from Nelly's in hand, and mumbled, "Bye y'all. See you soon."

"We will have fun at the Monster Bash!" Pearl called out as he shuffled down the sidewalk toward his little house.

When he was out of earshot, Rose Ellen sighed. "Thanks, Pearl, for picking up on that. I just couldn't face another night stuck with Kenny, especially after he bashed women."

"I don't know what's up with that. But, like we've talked about before, grief can cause a person to walk around with a dark cloud hanging over everything."

"Maybe, just maybe, Pearl, this dressing up and going to the Monster Bash might help him. He has taken a few steps forward lately."

"More like two steps forward and three steps back. He should be doing better by now."

Rose Ellen unlocked her door, kicked off her shoes and got two cold Dr. Peppers from the frig. She didn't have much room, but there was always enough space in her little refrigerator for their favorite drink.

"I just need a minute to re-group," she told Pearl. "Then we can see what we might be able to discover about the murder victims, and what else they had or didn't have in common."

She could see Pearl's eyes widen with excitement as she reached for her purse. "I just need some fresh lipstick."

Rose Ellen was beginning to think Pearl was addicted to the taste of her lipstick. Or maybe her obsession was based on the idea that she liked looking at herself in the mirror.

It had been a very stressful day, and Pearl's habit of constantly checking and reapplying her lipstick was starting to grind on Rose Ellen's frayed nerves.

Rose Ellen took a swig of her icy, liquid treat and instantly felt better. Nothing like a drink that was born in Texas to calm a body. She sighed and reminded herself that everyone had small, irritating habits.

She took another sip and thought about what a good person Pearl truly was, and that was what mattered. "You ready to do some research?"

"Sure, Ex. We might just get lucky and find something that has been overlooked."

Not likely, thought Rose Ellen. But it would be engaging to do some internet sleuthing. There had to be more connections between the victims of the Seventeen Dollar Murders.

They started their search by making a list of what they knew, or believed, like the fact that the three Tyler area women were baby boomers born between 1946 and 1964.

Two of the victims had been left near vacant stores, and another was placed in a field. All three had been strangled, stabbed and were holding seventeen dollars in cash when their bodies were found.

According to news stories, completed autopsy reports from the first two victims had not provided any additional information. There were no gunshot wounds, or evidence of other fatal injuries to the women. No foreign DNA was discovered on the bodies, as well.

Rose Ellen and Pearl decided that the method used most likely meant the same killer committed all three murders. They felt their original conclusion about the overkill aspect was correct, and did indeed signify a personal motive fueled by intense rage.

During their search, they discovered each victim had a Facebook page, but no friends in common. It didn't appear that they were interested in tweeting, and none had posted on a regular basis.

The murdered females all had some pictures on their Facebook pages, but most were group shots with grandkids. It was hard to tell, but Rose Ellen and Pearl noticed the women appeared to be short. Other than that, and their gray hair, the victims didn't really look alike.

"It's odd that we haven't run across these women at some point," Rose Ellen speculated as they looked at the photos of each woman. "I mean, Tyler does have around a hundred thousand people, so we don't know everybody. But being seniors, you'd think we would have crossed paths with at least one of them."

"What if they were the type that didn't get out and socialize? If you didn't live down the road from Kenny, we wouldn't know him."

"That's true. I hadn't thought of that, Pearl. You know, we should check the marital status of each woman."

Rose Ellen's heart rate escalated as she rapidly typed on her keyboard. "Check this out. I guess none of them were candidates for a Smith and Wesson divorce."

Pearl squinted and moved in for a closer look. "Okay, all three were widows who posted that their husbands died from natural causes."

"Look at this," she continued. "I don't remember the fact that they all lived alone being in the paper. That's not smart to post that fact these days. Could that have something to do with why they were targeted?"

"It makes you wonder. I agree with you about posting that you are alone, but I guess it wasn't important to report in the news, because most widows do live alone. And you know what the police do. They always hold back some details about the victims and the crimes," Rose Ellen said.

"Yes. That helps when they catch the criminal, because sometimes when they interrogate a suspect, he talks about some little something that only the guilty person would know. But why would their living arrangements be left out of news reports?"

"Maybe we just don't remember hearing that all were widows and lived by themselves, Pearl."

"You know, Ex, most people around here go to church. Let's see if any of them have something about that on their profiles."

"Great idea!" Rose Ellen began to look at each woman's personal information. Two didn't list a religion, but one did--Baptist.

Pearl sat up with a start. "Do you see what I see? Not only is she a Baptist, but that one woman is a member of the First Baptist Church—the same Baptist

Church Johnny Ray attends."

"That's weird. He never mentioned one of the victims was a member of his church."

"That is strange," Pearl added. "His congregation isn't that big. It's not like that Green Valley Baptist Church that has several thousand members. Johnny Ray would have at least known about this woman. You don't think…"

"Now, Pearl, there you go again getting all paranoid. You know darn well that Johnny Ray would never have a thing to do with anything this heinous."

"I know, but it does make you think. On some of those crime shows we watch, the perpetrator is the last person anyone would suspect. And think about this— we really don't know Johnny Ray that well."

Rose Ellen knew that was true. They had become acquainted with Johnny Ray recently at the Senior Society. But he couldn't be involved with such brutal murders. That was ridiculous. Still—it was odd that he had never mentioned the fact that he went to church with one of the dead women.

They continued searching in hopes they would discover the significance of the seventeen dollars. Was that number important to each homicide victim? Did the amount represent a cost? Did it have something to do with years or maybe ages? Or was the figure significant to the killer?

None of the victims' Facebook pages revealed anything remotely connected to that specific number. Why the women were all left clutching seventeen dollars in cash was still a mystery.

Rose Ellen pushed back from the computer, let out a big yawn and stretched her arms above her head. "I was kind of tired when we started this, and now I am dog tired. This was interesting, but I think I've had it for the day."

"Oh, that's catching, Ex," Pearl wearily uttered. She yawned and continued, "I'm tired, too. I think I'm ready to go home and get in my P.J.s, if you don't mind."

"That sounds good." Rose Ellen pictured herself curled up with Oscar in her *I Love Lucy* jammies. The set was almost in tatters, but she couldn't give up such comfortable pajamas.

"I'll pick you up about six day after tomorrow for the Monster Bash." Rose Ellen turned from the computer just in time to see Pearl holding her compact.

She puckered her freshly colored lips. "Okay, I'm ready now."

"Aren't you just going home to spend the evening alone? Good Grief. You don't need perfectly colored lips for that."

"True. But you never know what might happen on the way. If I got in an accident or something, I wouldn't want anyone to see me without my lipstick."

Seven

The Senior Society was unusually dark. Giant spiders tucked in cottony webs hung from the ceiling. A large, electronic witch cackled near the door, amid orange and black streamers. Seated in a chair nearby, was a life-sized skeleton wearing a purple top hat.

One of the main tables featured fall treats like Ruth's popcorn balls, candy corn, Peggy's Severed Finger Cookies and pumpkin pie. A smoke machine sent an eerie mist across the giant ghost centerpiece and a large bowl filled with orange-colored punch.

Strains of seasonal music like *The Monster Mash* greeted arriving guests, some of whom were barely recognizable behind their festive masks and wigs.

As they made their entrance, Rose Ellen felt optimistic about Kenny again. She had never seen him so excited. He had talked almost non-stop on their ride to the Senior Society about how perfect their costumes were for the event.

It was fun to see the variety of outfits donned by the party goers. There were the usual witches and ghosts, plus a few scarecrows. *The Wizard of Oz* was also represented by a Cowardly Lion.

Two women, who showed up in the same, exact saloon girl costumes, stared each other down. Their short, flirty skirts featured large petticoats and side slits almost to their hips.

"I don't think I'd be trying that, especially with those hooker hose," Rose Ellen whispered.

Kenny ignored her as they looked for an empty table. "This is great!"

His prospects for surviving grief were much better. It seemed like he had turned a corner. Maybe his negative attitude was a finally a thing of the past, and they wouldn't have to listen to comments about mean women anymore. Bess would be proud, Rose Ellen thought.

"Wow! You three look fantastic!" The trio turned around to see a woman dressed as a giant, glittering music note, standing next to a man donning a poster board with the words to *Flying Purple People Eater* scribbled across it.

"Peggy, is that you?" Rose Ellen asked.

"It's me and this is my friend, Bill. We are Melody and Lyric," the nonagenarian replied.

Bill nodded his head. "Pleased to meet you, musketeers."

"Good to meet you, also," Pearl responded. "I love your creativity. What a clever idea."

"It was Peggy's idea," Bill said, as he awkwardly tugged at the poster board hanging from his neck. "I don't think I can eat in this thing, though."

"No," Pearl laughed, "You'll want to get rid of that board before you try to eat any apple pie."

Melody and Lyric turned to greet other guests. "They have great costumes, but we look good, too, don't we?" Kenny beamed.

"I'd say we look pretty darn great, Kenny." Rose Ellen was more than happy to validate his enthusiasm.

Out of the corner of her eye, Rose Ellen spotted Ruth meekly standing by herself near the bathrooms. "She doesn't look right."

Pearl agreed. "Usually she's prissing around. And that God-awful hair is as flat as the panhandle. Most of the time, it looks like an oversized South Texas grapefruit sitting on top of her head. I think I can see some of her gray roots showing from way over here, too, bless her heart."

The three approached Ruth and greeted her. "Are you okay?" Pearl half-heartedly asked.

"I'm fine," Ruth stiffly replied. "I'm just not sure if I'm ready to face everyone, especially Nelda."

"Don't worry," Rose Ellen advised. "I think it has all been forgotten." But she didn't really believe the words as they tumbled out of her mouth.

Pearl lightly patted Ruth on the back, as Kenny tried to avoid being part of a potentially emotional discussion. "Well, we'd better mill around," he said.

Rose Ellen shot Pearl a "What's up with him?" look. She answered with a shrug, and *The Three Musketeers* walked away from a dejected looking Ruth.

"Would you look at that?" Kenny and Rose Ellen turned as Pearl pointed to a man dressed as the Devil. "You've got to be kidding me."

"Those costumes are unbelievable," the Devil exclaimed as he approached them. "I love the moustaches, and those curly wigs are so funny! You guys are perfect as *The Three Musketeers.*"

"Johnny Ray?" Rose Ellen looked surprised.

"In the flesh. The Devil himself."

"That's a good one Johnny Ray," Kenny added with a smile. "Being a preacher and all. I think it shows you have a good sense of humor."

Pearl and Rose Ellen stared at Kenny in disbelief.

Was this the same mousy loner that had looked on the dark side of everything since he lost his wife?

"I couldn't resist, Kenny. I guess I have always wanted to do something silly like this and never had the nerve. You know what they say about us seniors and a second childhood."

"Well, the way I look at it, if you haven't grown up by sixty, then you don't have to," Pearl said with a laugh.

"Just think about all the people older than that at the dances who still go out on the floor and do the Hokey Pokey."

"Whatever it is, I am enjoying some things about getting older, like the fact that I can be less serious and have fun with life," Johnny Ray added. "Speaking of having fun, I need to go network. Old habits die hard. I may be a retired preacher, but I still enjoy visiting with folks."

They watched his demon tail swing as he walked away, still a bit shocked at the fact that a preacher would dress as Lucifer.

"That's fun, but it's also kind of weird," Pearl commented.

"What do you mean?"

"Come on, Ex. Why would he dress like that? I mean just because someone is a preacher doesn't mean they can't be a bad person, or even a murderer."

"Would you please stop! I know we don't have violent crimes in Tyler very often, so we are all thrown by the Seventeen Dollar Murders. I realize we are a bit edgy and looking over our shoulders. But, really! Your suspicions are starting to become paranoid."

"Well, you never know," Pearl retorted, narrowing

her eyes. "Like you said, hiding in plain sight. That's what they are going to find out about those murders. The perpetrator is probably right under our noses. And when they catch him and it's somebody close to us, we'll see who was right to be suspicious."

"Let's eat. I'm starving!" Kenny interrupted.

It was perfect timing, thought Rose Ellen. There was no point in arguing with Pearl. It seemed like the recent gruesome events were making her almost delusional.

They found a table after helping themselves to fall treats like cornbread and beef stew, and the orange colored punch.

"What is this?" Pearl asked. "It's delicious."

"I don't know, but it sure is good. It tastes like a combination of orange soda and ginger ale," Rose Ellen added. "But there is something else in there I can't identify."

"I got the hot chocolate with those little marshmallows," Kenny said. "And I couldn't resist the desserts."

Pearl and Rose Ellen had indulged in some sweets, but Kenny's plate was laden with everything from pecan pie and lemon squares, to caramel cake and raisin bread pudding.

Kenny was doing well, thought Rose Ellen. He seemed more happy and relaxed than she had ever seen him. His hearty appetite was another good sign that things were looking up.

"I'm afraid I will spill something on this great costume," Pearl said as she took off her gloves and plumed hat. "I hope I don't drag my curly wig through whipped cream or something."

"Good idea," Kenny said, as he removed his musketeer hat and brushed back his fake curls. "We don't want to mess up these outfits before the contest. I just know we are going to win."

"I don't know. Melody and Lyric are pretty creative." Rose Ellen didn't want him to get his hopes built up too much. Secretly, she wished they would win. Not for the money, but for Kenny. He was on a slow roll, and first place in the costume contest would help him keep inching forward.

"Whatever the outcome, we are having a great time, and we do look fantastic!" Pearl exclaimed.

The three finished their goodies and headed for the trash bin with their empty paper plates, plastic cups and silverware.

"I think I will just go check my lipstick and make sure I get my hat back on right, before the contest begins," Pearl said.

Rose Ellen rolled her eyes at the thought of Pearl once again applying lipstick and puckering her lips into the Senior Society bathroom mirror.

Pearl made her way back to the table just in time to hear the Barrett Strong version of *Money (That's What I Want)*.

"I guess no band tonight, just that computerized music. But I like this recording better than the Beatles one," she whispered to Rose Ellen. She always enjoyed trying to get a rise out of the die-hard Beatles fan.

"Shhh!! They are getting ready to announce the top picks for the Almost Heaven Assisted Living Center Costume Contest," Kenny cautioned.

The contest was the highlight of the annual Senior Society Monster Bash. Each year, the competition got stiffer as the prize money was increased, and three hundred dollars could buy a lot of senior discount meals in Tyler, Texas.

The director of the assisted living center walked around the facility, eyeing the many creative outfits. It would be a tough decision, but she had to pick five finalists.

Costumes that were considered part of a group, like *The Three Musketeers,* were counted as one entry. Participants who made the final cut would then take the stage, and the audience would determine the winner.

It was no surprise when Melody and Lyric approached the stage, followed by a knight who struggled up the steps in his shiny suit of armor.

"Who is that, Ex?"

"I don't know. But who could tell? In that get-up, it could be a woman."

"The way he walks, I'm sure it's a man. But everyone we know is accounted for—I think. That's odd that some other new person is here, and no one bothered to introduce him. "

"Boy, I bet that suit is hot," Kenny commented.

"That's not hot," Pearl said, pointing across the room. "Holy Scarlet O'Hara! You talk about pushing the envelope. She just shoved it off the table, across the room and half way to Oklahoma. But why am I not surprised?"

Kenny and Rose Ellen turned to see what had caught Pearl's attention. And then they spotted Nelda in all her glory, dressed as Kim Kardashian.

"Ex, what on earth would possess her to dress like that at her age?"

"I don't know," Rose Ellen replied. She found it ironic that Pearl would make a comment about Nelda sporting an outfit that wasn't age appropriate.

Rose Ellen resisted the temptation to point out that fact and continued, "Maybe she thinks a tiny outfit, jewelry almost as big as one of her purses, and a dark wig jacked up to Jesus disguise her age."

"No way!" added Kenny. "She looks ridiculous...like a computer aged seventy-something Kim Kardashian. Only, I think Kim will end up looking better."

Pearl disgustedly folded her arms. "Apparently, she is fully recovered from the incident with Ruth. Too bad her boobs aren't as big as her purses, bless her heart."

Rose Ellen tried to suppress her giggles as the senior Kim Kardashian was summoned to the stage. Nelda confidently wiggled across the floor, totally unaware of the fact that with each bump and grind, there was a ripple of laughter.

She made a point to stop momentarily in front of Ruth, and gave her a glare that was as blistering as a hot, South Texas wind. Ruth quickly lowered her head as Nelda gyrated her way toward the spotlight.

The senior Kim Kardashian stood proudly next to Melody, Lyric and the unfamiliar knight. The announcement was made: "And now for number four...the Devil!!"

Johnny Ray waved to the cheering audience as he joined the group of finalists. His tail swung wildly and hit Nelda--aka Kim--in her padded, big butt. Nelda playfully winked, and Johnny Ray turned as red as his costume.

"Oh, boy. It doesn't look like we will be included," Kenny sighed.

The director of the Almost Heaven Assisted Living Center breathlessly announced, "And now for the fifth and final contestant...or should I say contestants... in our costume contest...*The Three Musketeers!*"

Rose Ellen and Pearl almost had to gallop to keep up with Kenny as he ran toward the stage. They all adjusted their large, plumed hats and curly wigs, and Pearl dramatically held out her cape.

"Now," said the director, "for the winner. I will hold my hand above each finalist or finalists, and you will clap to indicate which will take home our three-hundred-dollar prize!"

Melody and Lyric got a moderate amount of applause, along with the knight, who was tottering under the weight of his costume. Nelda swiveled her hips and got a few polite claps.

The crowd roared when the director held her hand over Johnny Ray's Devil horns. He grinned and triumphantly raised his crimson pitchfork above his head.

"I don't see how we can beat that," Pearl whispered.

Rose Ellen sucked in her stomach and took a deep breath. "Here we go."

The assisted living center director moved her hand over the trio. The three were overwhelmed as booming applause thundered through the Senior Society, followed by several enthusiastic, loud whistles.

"The winner of this year's Almost Heaven Assisted Living Center Costume Contest is... *The*

Three Musketeers!"

"Take the money, Kenny," Rose Ellen urged. "We did it!"

Kenny proudly held up three crisp, one hundred dollar bills as cell phones flashed around the room. How wonderful, thought Rose Ellen. It was just what Kenny needed.

They made their way back to the table though a throng of well-wishers. Rose Ellen had to admit to herself that it was exciting to be the center of attention. Not to mention the fact that they were each one hundred dollars richer.

"Now we can take off some of this stuff, Ex. It's hot and heavy."

"I'm heading to the bathroom," Kenny said.

"We can at least shed a few pieces, like our hats, wigs and gloves," added Pearl. "I hope my hair isn't too messed up."

"It will be okay," Rose Ellen responded. She removed her plumed hat and wig and shook her head. "Oh, I feel much better now...and lighter! The knight definitely needs to lighten his load, too. Hey, where is he?"

"Maybe he is upset that he didn't win. I don't see him."

"I bet he went to the bathroom to get out of that armor, and put on something more comfortable," Kenny added, as he made his way to the men's room.

"Something must be wrong with their smoke machine. It seems really foggy in here," Pearl commented.

Rose Ellen sniffed the air. "It smells funny, too. Is something burning?"

Someone reached behind the smoke machine and unplugged it. But the room continued to fill with a thick haze.

Suddenly, the smoke alarms blared. People began to cough, and Rose Ellen's eyes started to burn.

"Fire! Get out!" somebody in the crowd warned.

"Ex, it isn't the smoke machine! It's a fire. Let's go!"

"We have to find Kenny," Rose Ellen gasped.

As they approached the men's room the smoke became thicker, and they both coughed continuously, as they fought their way to the door. Flames licked the walls, making it obvious that the fire had probably been set in the bathroom.

"Kenny!" Pearl screamed "If you are in there, come on! We have to get out."

Rose Ellen choked and suddenly felt like she was on top of an angry, bucking bull. The room began spinning and everything was turning gray.

Pearl tried to catch her as she fell to her knees near the door. But her efforts were fruitless, and Rose Ellen crumpled on to the floor.

"Wake up, Ex. We have to go!"

She frantically tried to pull Rose Ellen from the entrance as a man whose head was covered with what appeared to be damp paper towels pushed past them. But it wasn't Kenny.

Was it the man who had been dressed as a knight? If so, where was his armor? Pearl quickly decided there was no time to think about that. And if Kenny was still trapped, she would try to help him later. Her immediate concern was getting her best friend to safety.

Pearl reluctantly gave Rose Ellen a slap. She opened her eyes as Pearl screamed again, "Come on! You have to get up!"

Rose Ellen saw a strange, dark shadow emerge from the blazing bathroom. She blinked her eyes, attempting to fight off the wooziness.

The figure was a man who had a large piece of material draped around his upper body. She felt water dripping on her face as he leaned over, and realized it was coming from his wet clothing.

Rose Ellen felt something pulling her up. "What's going on?"

The shadowy figure wrapped his arms around her and the soaking wet cloth fell over her. She shivered from the cold as it hit her with a thud. She looked up and saw horns on top of the strange creature's head.

She felt Pearl try to grab her hand, but it slipped from her grasp. Then the eerie form carried the helpless Rose Ellen away from the fiery room.

"Oh, no. I died, didn't I? I'm dead. Was I that bad?" Rose Ellen mumbled. "Am I going down there?"

"You're okay. Everything is going to be all right. It's me, Johnny Ray."

Eight

Rose Ellen sighed with contentment. She stroked Oscar, who slept peacefully on her chest. It was true—there was no place like home. After a check-up at the hospital, she had, thankfully, been released.

The events at the Monster Bash still lingered in her mind as she relaxed on her couch. Rose Ellen was grateful that Johnny Ray had saved her from what could have been a terrible fate.

After realizing he was in a burning bathroom, Johnny Ray had quickly soaked his upper body and cape with water, so he could more easily escape the fiery trap.

Tears came to her eyes when she realized Pearl had never left her side during the entire ordeal. What a rare, loyal friend.

What happened? Did someone deliberately set the fire in the men's room? Was it the killer, and was the fire connected to the Seventeen Dollar Murders?

First responders sometimes came to the Senior Society for incidents like a possible heart attack. But the occurrence with Nelda and Ruth was a first. Now this, Rose Ellen thought. In all the years that she had been going to the society, there had never been a fire and only a few false alarms.

What was going on? Their wonderful little city was dealing with three unsolved homicides, and now a fire that appeared to have been set on purpose.

Tyler, Texas, was all about seniors. The retirement

town had often boasted in news releases that it "celebrated seniors." Residents faithfully read the *Seniorific News* and looked forward to activities geared toward baby boomers and older seniors. It was a safe, happy place for people to spend their golden years.

Rose Ellen wiped a tear away with the back of her hand. How could someone in their hometown do these things? And why?

She thought about Pearl's suspicion concerning Johnny Ray. If he was the murderer, why would he have made such an effort to save her from the fire? Was that just a smoke screen to throw everyone off?

That was absurd. Or was it? It still bothered her that he had not ever mentioned the fact that one of the victims was a member of his congregation at The First Baptist Church.

Kenny had been in the bathroom too, right before the fire. Surely, he wouldn't have done anything so horrible. Where was he when they tried to find him?

Rose Ellen thought about Bill—Peggy's friend and musical costume partner. Could the man who dressed as Lyric be a killer, or a pyromaniac? He was new in their group, and no one knew much about him.

Bill was as old as Peggy. Someone in his nineties wouldn't have the physical strength to viciously strangle and stab three younger women, and then move the bodies. It was doubtful he had started the fire, also.

What about Nelda? Did she blame the Senior Society for the fight with Ruth? Was she so angry about losing the costume contest that she sneaked into the men's room and lit a match?

And then there was Ruth. Like Nelda, she probably didn't commit the recent homicides, but what about the arson? Was she so humiliated that she wanted to get back at Nelda and the seniors who witnessed their fight?

Why was Ruth hanging out by the Senior Society bathrooms early in the evening? Did she do something to start a slow burning fire? Was it really an arson? It was possible that the fire was just an accident.

What about the stranger that came to the Monster Bash as the knight? Who was he? And was he the man who ran out of the bathroom?

Just about everyone was taken to St. Joseph hospital for observation, and thank goodness, there were no serious injuries. Like Rose Ellen, most had been treated for smoke inhalation and released.

She didn't recall seeing the man dressed like a knight at the hospital. Had he set the fire, shed his armor and then left before it became an inferno? Or was it a man?

A thousand questions bombarded her mind. She just wanted to close her eyes and make everything bad that had happened simply go away. Why couldn't life magically return to the way it was before—peaceful and quiet?

Rose Ellen held tightly to Oscar. There was nothing like a pet to make you feel like everything was going to be all right.

Oscar jumped at the sound of a rap on the door. "Hey, Ex, can I come in?"

Rose Ellen reluctantly gave up her spot on the couch to her feline and opened the door to greet Pearl.

"Sure. You are always welcome."

Pearl stood holding a huge pot. "Thought you might need some homemade soup after what you've been through, and you probably don't feel like fixing supper."

"Thanks, but I'm not sick. And the fire at the Senior Society was hard on you, too."

"Okay. Let's both have some soup, then."

Rose Ellen had to admit that a big bowl of hot soup sounded wonderful. Like a faithful pet, homemade soup could also make the world seem right again.

Pearl put the pot on a burner and hesitated. "You know, I thought I was going to lose you. I'm so glad you are okay, and they don't think you will have any lasting effects from the smoke."

"Me, too. I just don't understand why it hit me so much harder than it hit you."

"Everybody's different, hon. Who knows? I was so relieved when Johnny Ray came out of the fire and took us to a safe place. When he grabbed you up in his arms, he told me to hold on to his Devil tail. I couldn't see, and I really don't know if I could have gotten out without him and that crazy tail."

"So, that's why you let go of my hand?"

"Yes. I'm thankful for his guidance. He knew what to do to get us out of there."

"I'm thankful, too, for all the young volunteers that are going to help fix the damage to the Senior Society. So many people depend on the services they provide, and that will help them get up and running a lot faster."

"Yes," replied Pearl. "We have to be grateful for the good people in our world. We may have a murderer in our midst, but we are also surrounded by a lot of wonderful folks."

Pearl slowly stirred the soup. The aroma of chicken and vegetables filled the tiny house kitchen, and suddenly Rose Ellen felt very hungry.

"You know, Ex, we were the generation that was going to change the world, remember?"

"I remember. And we didn't trust anyone over thirty."

Pearl laughed. "That's right. But I've been thinking. Maybe we didn't change the world, but we have a chance now to try to help our little corner."

"What do you mean?"

"Now don't get on me, but what would it hurt to pursue our ideas a little bit more? Maybe we could help. I mean, three murders and now a fire that could have killed us all? We have more time than law enforcement to just piddle around on the internet some more and see what we can find."

Pearl had always been persuasive, but this time Rose Ellen had to agree with her. They could just sit back and wait for the next terrible incident to occur, or they could try to do something to prevent more possible deaths.

There was a good chance they wouldn't be able to add anything to the murder investigation, or connect the homicides to the fire, but why not give it another try?

"Sounds good to me," Rose Ellen responded. "Maybe for now, we could just concentrate on the murders."

"Yes, one step at a time. The Seventeen Dollar Murders are more pressing, and we might find something that ties those crimes and the fire together."

The two revisited what they had already

uncovered. All three casualties were baby boomers and widows who lived alone. They had suffered very "up close and personal" deaths by strangulation and were victims of postmortem stabbing. Other than those facts, it didn't appear that they had much in common.

They stuck to their theory that only one killer was involved, even though it was still remotely possible—like they had speculated before, that one person committed the first homicide, and the other two were copycat killers.

The killer or killers could have been female, but it was unlikely. Most women would not have the physical strength to overpower their prey and deal with the bodies. At least not without help.

With so little blood at the murder scenes, it was apparent all three had been killed somewhere else and dumped where they were eventually found. Did that mean something?

Pearl brought two bowls of soup to Rose Ellen's little table, and they sat in silence for a few minutes as they sipped the steaming broth.

"This is so good, Pearl. Thank you. It's just what I needed."

"You're welcome. It does seem to hit the spot, doesn't it? It's just another reason why I love this time of year. Hey, by the way, what are you going to do for Thanksgiving?"

"Wow. That is just a few weeks away, isn't it? I guess the usual. I will spend the day with Jennifer and her family. I miss the times when the grandkids were younger. Now they are so busy, we are lucky if they sit at the table for a few minutes—even for a holiday meal."

"I know what you mean, Ex. And if they do, they are playing on their phones while they eat. It seems like our kids and grandkids don't have much time for us anymore—just their phones. Everybody is so busy. I imagine I will end up eating at one of my boys' houses. I appreciate being asked, but it just seems like we rush through those meals. I miss the old days with everyone visiting at the table and no technical interruptions."

Perhaps, thought Rose Ellen, that was another reason she and her ex-sister-in-law were so bonded. It wasn't that their kids and grandkids didn't love them. Life was so much more complicated and hectic for younger generations. Pearl and Rose Ellen gave each other the attention their families often didn't have time to provide.

"It's sad, but true. There are too many distractions these days." Rose Ellen took another mouthful of soup. "Mmm. This is just so yummy."

"I just thought of something," Pearl interrupted. "Back to our search--you know on that episode of *Homicide Hunter*, Lt. Joe Kenda said something about JDLR and how it was police code for Just Doesn't Look Right? Maybe we should approach our search like that."

"That's a good idea, Pearl. We can consider things that just don't look right. Like Lt. Kenda said, sometimes detectives have no proof, but their instincts tell them something isn't right about a person or some detail about the crime. I have a feeling that the homicides and the fire at the Senior Society aren't connected."

"I'm leaning that way, too. It also doesn't look

right to me that all three murder victims were women, who were apparently not robbed and none were sexually assaulted. But then older women aren't usually victims of those kinds of violent crimes. Why were they killed so viciously?"

"I'm not sure," added Rose Ellen. "I wonder about the seventeen dollars in cash left at each scene. I know we have tried that angle before, but maybe we can think of another way to look at that clue."

"You know what? You can find anyone's marriage date easily. It's a matter of public record. Do you think any of them were married seventeen years, and that is why that amount was left with the victims?"

"I don't know what made you think of that, Pearl, but that's a good idea. Off the wall, but good."

Pearl cleared the dishes while Rose Ellen turned on her computer. She pulled up the articles about the homicides and quickly jotted down each woman's full name.

"Maybe we'll get lucky and find out they all married in Texas," said Rose Ellen. "That would sure narrow down our search."

She located a large data base for Texas marriages and typed in the first name of each victim under "Brides" and the last names under "Grooms." Luck was with them. All three had married in The Lone Star State.

Rose Ellen then discovered the tombstones for the three deceased husbands on findagrave.com, and subtracted marriage dates from death dates.

"Well, the first one was married thirty-four years, not seventeen," Rose Ellen reported as she continued to search.

"This is interesting. The next one was also married thirty-four years."

"Ex, didn't Kenny ask you how long you had been married, and then he acted kind of funny when you told him thirty-four years?"

"Yes. But I imagine that's just a coincidence. Oh wow! Look—the third victim was also married thirty-four years. Now, that's probably not a coincidence."

Maybe the police already knew that all three victims—on top of a few other similarities—had been married thirty-four years. Perhaps they had explored that as being significant, but that fact was not in any article about the crimes, either.

Excited about their first real lead, the two amateur detectives continued to search for other clues. They tried to dig up anything they could to tie the exact number of years each victim had been married to seventeen.

"I don't think we are getting anywhere, Pearl." Rose Ellen pushed back her chair and looked at her watch. "We've been at this for over an hour. I don't know about you, but I could use a cold Dr. Pepper right now."

Pearl got up and retrieved two sodas. She headed back to the table and suddenly stopped. "You know…thirty-four divided by two is seventeen."

"Yeah. But what would that have to do with anything?"

"I'm not sure. I guess after all this boomer/senior sleuthing, that is the only thing I could come up with to tie the two figures together."

"Well, Pearl, it's an unusual idea. I'm just not sure where we would go with that."

"You are right. Let's take a break. Where's that great Ricky Skaggs CD you bought?"

Rose Ellen reached into a drawer under the coffee table. Nothing was very far away in a tiny house, and it was hard to lose anything in such a small area.

"Here it is. *Music to My Ears.* It's a great bluegrass collection," Rose Ellen commented, as she popped it in the player. "I also bought a good one by that young group of pickers, Flatt Lonesome. I'll play that CD for you, sometime, too."

The two sat down beside Oscar, who was still snoozing on the couch. They sipped their Dr. Peppers and began to tap their toes with the lively music.

"That song is hilarious," Rose Ellen giggled, as they listened to *You Can't Hurt Ham.*

"Here's my favorite part, except I can't remember all of the words," Pearl said, as she tried to sing along with Ricky Skaggs:

You can hurt potato salad and it can hurt you back.

Get a hold of milk too old and throw things outta whack...

There's a culinary promise that's known throughout the land

No frigerate; No expire date. You know, you can't hurt ham.

"It's funny and it's true," said Rose Ellen. "If it's country ham that has been cured the old-fashioned way, it will pretty much last longer than we will!"

"This is a great diversion, Ex. I mean, not just from our search, but from all the madness that seems to have taken over our lives lately."

"Nothing like a good, old bluegrass tune to

brighten your spirits, huh?" Rose Ellen asked.

"You got that right. Makes me feel like dancing a jig, like my Kentucky born Granny used to do. She always told me that bluegrass was a combination of influences from places like Ireland and Scotland. It kind of took on a life of its own in Appalachia, when folks like her people settled there."

Pearl jumped up and began to dance, laughing as she bumped into the small coffee table. "Not so easy in a tiny house!"

Still a little weak from her ordeal at the Senior Society, Rose Ellen remained seated and clapped in time with the music as Pearl kicked up her heels.

Oscar raised his head and meowed his disgust. He looked at Rose Ellen as if to say, "Who's house is this anyway? How dare you interrupt my nap!"

"Turn off the music. I think my phone is ringing." Rose Ellen requested, as she reached for it.

"Oh, hi, Kenny. How are you?" Rose Ellen rolled her eyes "Now? Well, to be honest, now is not a good time. I'm still kind of wiped out from the fire and all. I'm fine, but I have a few lingering, temporary effects from the smoke inhalation."

She sighed. "Yes, Pearl's here, but she just came by to bring me some soup."

She looked at Pearl helplessly and tried to politely discourage Kenny. "Pearl's leaving in just a few minutes, and then I'm probably going to turn in early tonight."

Rose Ellen clapped her hand over the phone and mouthed, "You can stay as long as you want."

Pearl nodded and whispered, "Doesn't he know how to take a hint?"

Rose Ellen frowned. "Kenny, really. I'm just so tired. I don't feel like company, and as I said, Pearl isn't staying. Why don't we all plan to go out to lunch in a few days? How would that be?"

Pearl could tell from the look on her face that Rose Ellen was getting really irritated. Kenny was determined to make a nuisance of himself. The worst part about it was he didn't see himself as a nuisance at all.

"Yes, maybe tomorrow. Let me wait and see how I feel."

Rose Ellen clenched her fist. "No, Kenny, I can't tell you for sure right now!"

"Tell him you have another call," Pearl advised.

"Kenny, I have to go. I'm getting another call. Okay. But make it quick. What do you need to ask me?"

Pearl saw Rose Ellen's face turn pale and heard her say, "What was that, Kenny?" Rose Ellen leaned into Pearl so she, too, could hear Kenny repeat his request.

"Would you go out with me, Rose Ellen?"

"You mean on a date, Kenny?"

"Yes, a date."

Rose Ellen's eyes widened and the words carelessly spilled out of her mouth before she could stop them. "Oh, crap!"

Nine

"Is that what you think of going out with me, Rose Ellen?" It almost sounded like Kenny had started to cry.

"Oh, no, Kenny. I'm sorry. I said, 'Oh, crap' because it took me by surprise. I thought we were just friends. I never expected you to ask me for a date."

"What's wrong with that?"

"Nothing. Nothing at all. And I didn't mean going out with you was crap. Like I said, I didn't expect you to ask me to go out."

"So--you won't?"

Rose Ellen struggled to find the right words. "I think any woman would be lucky to have a date with you. It's just that I'm not interested in dating anyone. You can ask Pearl."

Pearl affirmatively shook her head. "Kenny, have you ever known me to go out with anyone?" Rose Ellen continued.

"Well, we haven't been acquainted that long." Acquainted? Rose Ellen felt like he was using a more formal word to impress her and possibly sway her decision in his direction.

She hesitated, and then pressed on. "I know, but I am happy with my life. Since my divorce, I have been content to just enjoy being friends with any man I know."

"But women are supposed to be with a man romantically."

Rose Ellen bit her tongue. She wanted to say something like, "Says who?" But she took a deep breath and replied, "I guess I might think the way I do because I was romantically involved with someone, and it didn't last."

Pearl frowned and Rose Ellen quickly added, "I mean I'm happy I had that time in my life. It was good, and I have my daughter Jennifer because of that relationship. But now, I am perfectly content being on my own."

Pearl made a slicing motion across her neck. "He's being rude, so be rude back!" She said it loudly, hoping Kenny would hear her comment and recognize the fact that he was being pushy.

"Kenny! I have to go. I missed a call, and it was someone I needed to talk to," Rose Ellen lied. "I need to call them back. No! It wasn't a man! And even if it was, it's none of your business!" She disgustedly pressed the screen and cut him off.

"I thought things were better with him, Ex."

"Me, too. It seems like being nice to him just got me in hot water."

"Well, you tried. Who would have thought the little wuss who rarely left his house would now decide he is a Casanova?"

"Was I too nice, Pearl?"

"No. Well, maybe a little nicer than I would have been. You certainly didn't send him any wrong signals. And like you said, you never felt any romantic vibes from him, either."

"I sure didn't see this coming, Pearl. I feel sorry for him, but enough is enough. I'm done trying to fix Kenny."

"You did all you could, hon." Pearl reached out and gently patted Rose Ellen's back. "Sometimes, no matter how hard you try, you just can't make things better for someone else. People have to do that on their own."

She was right. Still, Rose Ellen couldn't help feeling badly for him. "It must have been hard for him to lose Bess."

"I know, but think about this. It's hard enough to lose someone to illness, like Kenny did. But the families of the murder victims had to lose their loved ones violently. To make matters worse, no one knows who did it or why. That's who I really feel sorry for."

Rose Ellen shuddered as she thought about the families of the Seventeen Dollar Murder victims. She wished there was a way she could help people like that who had truly been devastated and hurt.

It bothered her that, even though it wasn't nearly as traumatic, she had upset Kenny. Hurt or not, though, she was going to have to stand strong and refuse his advances.

"I don't think lunch is such a good idea, Pearl. I'm afraid that would send the wrong message. It might be best to cut as many ties as possible with Kenny."

"You're right. It sounds like he made it very clear he wanted a romantic relationship with you. It would just encourage him if you included him in social things anymore—even with me along."

Rose Ellen looked at her Dr. Pepper. "I wish this was straight Jack Daniels," she said, taking a big gulp. "I need a shot of courage for what I am about to do."

"I can fix that," Pearl said with a laugh.

"That's okay. I need to have a clear head for this."

Rose Ellen's hand was visibly shaking as she slowly tapped the screen of her phone. Pearl gave her a nod, as if to say, "Go ahead. You have to do this. It's the right thing."

The only word Kenny managed to get out was "Hello" before Rose Ellen's phrases spewed forth like boiling, hot water from a garden hose on a scorching, summer day. She informed him that they could no longer see each other without other people around, and explained it was apparent they wanted different things.

She knew she had to be firm, but tried to handle his feelings as gently as possible. That was a challenge with a man like Kenny. In some ways, he seemed very sensitive. But then the "all about me" side made it hard to get through to him. Rose Ellen had learned that Kenny wasn't good about accepting other people's opinions, if they disagreed with his.

Of course—Rose Ellen told him--they could be cordial at social events, and he was welcome to sit at their table. But he could not come over and watch TV anymore, and they would not be going out to lunch together--ever.

Kenny angrily let her know that it was a romantic relationship or nothing. "If that's the way you feel, then you can forget being friendly! The next time I see you, I will turn around and walk the other way. I can't believe you did this to me!"

Rose Ellen hung up the phone and broke down. "I hate hurting someone."

"I know, sweetie. But you can't continue to have a friendly relationship with a man who wants something more. It's like dangling a carrot in front of a hungry rabbit and then jerking it out of reach. That's really hurtful. This way you yanked the band aid off, and it was quick, and in the long run, less painful."

"You want to look some more for clues?" Rose Ellen sniffed.

"No, I think it's time for you to rest. But I find it fascinating to try to figure out a murder mystery. I always thought I'd be a good detective."

Rose Ellen had to admit that, even though she had her doubts about Pearl's obsession with solving the crimes and becoming boomer/senior sleuths, she, too, was intrigued by their search.

"Pearl, dreams don't have an expiration date. You could still do something like detective work. Remember the folk artist Grandma Moses? She didn't paint in earnest until she was seventy-eight-years old. She ended up with an exhibit at the Museum of Modern Art in New York and two honorary doctoral degrees."

"And what about that bridge player at the Senior Center?" Rose Ellen continued. "What's her name…Kathy? She raised a family and then went on to become a flight attendant at almost sixty. It's never too late to chase a dream."

"Maybe you are right. I guess it wouldn't hurt to at least check out some courses at Tyler Junior College."

"Oh, let's look!" Rose Ellen suggested.

"No, I think it's time for me to go home. It's getting late."

"Honestly, Pearl. I don't want you to go. I need a diversion to get my mind off Kenny. I know I did the right thing, but I still feel badly."

Rose Ellen sat down and began to click her fingers

on the computer keyboard. She pulled up the Tyler Junior College website and discovered a lot of courses that might interest Pearl.

"Wow!" Pearl exclaimed. "I didn't know they had certificate programs. They list alternatives to full-fledged associate degree programs that wouldn't take that much time—since I don't have as much as I did forty years ago."

Rose Ellen began to relax as they scrolled through details about various criminal justice courses, like Crime in America and Police Systems and Practices. It lifted her spirits to watch Pearl's enthusiasm as they explored various options the college had to offer.

"Who knows, I might even open my own private detective agency. I could put the words 'Boomer/Senior Sleuth' under my name on the door. Well, not really," Pearl giggled. "It would be fun, though, to take a few of those courses just for the heck of it. I'm going to seriously check that out."

"Good grief," Rose Ellen said. "Every time I try to do anything on the computer, those stupid dating websites pop up. It's irritating."

"Ex, that's it! Why don't we check out that website for people over fifty? Let's see if any of the victims were on that mature dating one we see advertised all the time. I mean, if you are up to it."

"Sure," Rose Ellen replied. "Let's see what we can find." She turned her attention back to the screen and quickly found online newspaper articles that featured numerous headshots of the victims, before they were murdered.

Armed with those and their names, Rose Ellen began to search for their profiles on the most popular dating site for older adults.

"Bingo! Here's the first one, Pearl. That widow was looking for dates."

"This is exciting, Ex. We may have uncovered a good clue."

"I'd say so. Look at this! The second one also has a profile on the same website."

Rose Ellen's fingers flew as she typed in the third victim's name. Like she did with the other two, she added the words "Tyler, Texas." She wanted to be sure she had the right person and not some similar looking woman with the same name, who lived halfway across the country.

"How weird," Pearl commented. "All three victims were on the same dating website. Do you think the cops know this?"

"I don't know. You'd think they would, but maybe not. I think we are definitely getting somewhere, now."

Rose Ellen and Pearl suddenly turned and looked at each other in amazement. "Are you thinking what I'm thinking?" Pearl gasped.

"Kenny!" they blurted out together.

Rose Ellen tried to steady her hands as they trembled in anticipation. Could it be that Kenny was on the same website? Surely not, she thought. He was such a loner and didn't seem the type to have a profile on a mature dating website.

But then, she hadn't recognized his romantic interest. How well did she and Pearl know Kenny, anyway?

"Holy Scarlet O'Hara, Pearl!!"

"Holy Scarlet O'Hara and Rhett Butler, too!" Pearl yelled back.

There it was. A photo of Kenny wearing a black cowboy hat, bolo tie and a fancy, western shirt. He was posed with his arms crossed in a macho stance, and had a grin that came across as a smug, overly confident sneer.

The face was the same, but the attitude displayed in the picture was something they had never seen. He was trying to portray himself as a Texas stud, but he looked more like a drugstore cowboy with a big hat and no cattle.

"What does he say about himself? Are you sure it's our Kenny in Tyler?"

"Yes, Pearl. It says right here that's where he lives and it's his photo. Let's see…"

Rose Ellen scrolled down the page as Pearl leaned in for a better view.

I love a good time and I'm full of surprises. Give me a chance, and I'll take you on the ride of your life. If you are into rough and ready guys, I'm your man. I am a proud, wild and western resident of the Lone Star State. But don't let that fool you. I can also be as gentle as a lamb in the bedroom.

"Whoa! Hold your horses!" Rose Ellen's eyes were as wide as the state of Texas. "Is this the same Kenny? The wimpy one we know never had any dirt on his boots, let alone mud on his tires."

"Holy cow, Ex! It's almost like Dr. Jekyll and Mr. Hyde. The man we thought we knew is a big you-know-what. If there was a definition in old Mr. Webster's book for him, it would say 'lily livered mama's boy.' But this Kenny is trying to come off as self-assured and seems to think he is God's gift to women."

"I just can't believe it's the same guy. Remember what we said about hiding in plain sight? You don't think…" Rose Ellen stopped in mid-sentence.

"That all three murder victims had hooked up with Kenny?"

"I don't know that we can tell that without actually joining the website. But you know, it would be worth passing this information along to the police."

"Would they take us seriously?"

"Maybe not. But what would it hurt? They might already have this information. If they don't, why not let them know what we found out? It doesn't mean Kenny is the murderer. I just can't picture that. But it's more than a coincidence that all three victims are on the same mature, dating website with him."

"Ex, you are right. Kenny may be weird and obviously has two sides, but I can't imagine him committing such vicious acts as the Seventeen Dollar Murders. I know we don't know him as well as we thought…but… really."

"I just don't think it's possible that Kenny is a murderer, either. Being needy or different doesn't make you bad. And having a secret life doesn't necessarily mean you are evil."

"That's true," said Pearl, "But this is pretty strange. It's too late now, but tomorrow morning bright and early, I think I will go into the police station and let them know what we discovered. The worst thing they can do is laugh at me. I have stopped caring about what people think of me. That's a big advantage of growing older. You finally become comfortable just being yourself and speaking your mind."

"That's a good idea." Rose Ellen responded as she

thought about the fact that Pearl had never really cared about what anyone else thought of her. "This may be nothing, and it's probably just a strange coincidence that won't add anything to their investigation. But we do have an obligation to report what we found."

"Whew. Now, I'm the one that's tired, Ex."

"Yes, I'm ready to rest now. This has been an exhausting couple of weeks, for sure. Our little discovery about Kenny has made me want to grab Oscar and pile up in the bed with him under my Grandma's old quilt."

"Sounds great. It's time to hit the hay. I think I'll head home. Like you said, a nice warm bed sounds pretty good right now."

The two exchanged hugs and Pearl headed for the door. "Let's do lunch, okay? Well...without Kenny!"

"It's a date!" Rose Ellen called out as she heard her front door shut. She began to clean up and had almost finished loading her little dishwasher, when she realized the front door was unlocked.

As she started to turn the deadbolt, Rose Ellen saw lights shining through the window. Pearl's car was still in front of her tiny house with the engine running. Did Pearl's cell phone ring?

Was she calling for help because something was wrong with her car? If must be okay, Rose Ellen decided. Maybe she was just warming up her vehicle. But it wasn't that cold outside. Besides that, if she had a problem, she would have just come back inside.

Suddenly, the car lights went out, and Rose Ellen saw Pearl emerge from the driver's side. It looked like someone had walked up beside her, and they were both coming back to the house.

As the pair approached the front door, Rose Ellen could see in the glow of her porch light that it was Kenny. What was he doing? Why was he with Pearl? Did something happen and he needed their help?

She nervously flung the door open and couldn't believe what she was witnessing.

"Let us in now, and don't make a sound!" Kenny demanded.

Rose Ellen was dumbfounded. Kenny's eyes were almost black and evil looking. His voice was more than menacing—it was downright terrifying.

And then she saw it. A shiny knife blade was pressed up against Pearl's throat. "Do what he says." Pearl struggled to get the words out as Kenny pushed her inside.

He slammed the door shut with his foot and wheeled around. "You're both going to get it, now! You see what you have done, Rose Ellen? It was going to be just you. But now your stupid friend is going to be dead, too. She was checking her lipstick, like the floozy that she is and saw me in her visor mirror."

He took a ragged breath and continued. "Too bad for her she still has good eyesight, and she spotted me behind the car in the dark. I was waiting until she pulled away, so I could catch you alone, but eagle eyes here messed things up!"

He jerked Pearl forward, careful not to drop the knife, and her fearful eyes widened. Rose Ellen recalled the many times Pearl had bragged about her night vision and how good it was for someone over sixty.

"Why was she still here anyway? You lied, Rose Ellen. You said she was leaving, and you didn't want company. Why is she good enough for you, but not me?"

Rose Ellen tried to respond, but words wouldn't come out. Everything was happening in slow motion and nothing seemed real. Kenny momentarily lowered the knife.

Pearl looked at Rose Ellen apologetically. "I thought I spotted something behind my car, so I turned around and looked. Then I saw Kenny with a big knife coming up beside my door," she whispered. "I'm sorry, Ex. I should have just let him take me."

"Oh no!" Kenny continued to rant. "I would have gotten this tramp anyway." He raised the knife and pointed it at Rose Ellen.

He quickly put it back up against Pearl's throat. "This dumb heifer was trying to call for help. Well, it's too late now. Nobody can help you two."

He raised the knife again and shouted, "They are going to find you just like the others, and nobody will ever know that your pitiful little voices begged for mercy during your last moments on earth. No one will ever know what happened as you died---except for me!"

Ten

The fear and terror were paralyzing. Rose Ellen desperately tried to think. What could she do? If she went for the knife, or Kenny, he might slit Pearl's throat. She couldn't offer to change places with his captive. He had already made it clear that both women were going to be killed.

Could she make it to her cell phone and call for help? She probably couldn't risk that, either. What if she screamed? In the Tiny House Village, homes were close to each other, so neighbors would probably hear her and come immediately to offer their assistance. Would that infuriate Kenny enough to stab Pearl before help arrived?

Rose Ellen remembered what a survivor had said on one of their favorite crime shows about how she tried to make her attacker calm down. Maybe that would work, and Kenny would relax enough for them to run for help.

He hadn't locked the door when he kicked it shut. In her little house, the front door wasn't that far from where they were standing. Could she and Pearl make it out? Or would he catch them and viciously use the knife he was wielding?

"K... K...Kenny," she stuttered. Words were finally emerging from her lips. "Can we talk?"

"It's too late for that, Rose Ellen! You had your chance, and you turned out like all the rest. You taunt a man and then throw him away like trash."

"I never meant to do anything, but be your friend. Why are you doing this?"

"I told you!" he screamed. "You and the other ones are evil liars. They got what they deserved, and you will, too."

Rose Ellen was horrified as the reality of the situation sunk in. Kenny had committed three homicides. He was the Seventeen Dollar Murderer. How could that be possible?

"I didn't mean to lie," Rose Ellen hesitantly continued. "I'm sorry. I thought you just wanted to be friends. Please forgive me if I did or said anything that led you to believe we could be romantically involved."

"You know what you did. Just like Bess and the others. You make a man feel like he is special, and then you pull the rug right out from underneath him."

Rose Ellen's head was spinning. What did Kenny mean about Bess? He had always indicated that they had a loving relationship. What happened? Did she dare ask him?

She gulped and took a chance. "I'm sorry. Did Bess hurt you, Kenny? I hope not. You are such a sweet person. You don't deserve to be hurt."

"Shut up! You knew what you were doing. You planned to hurt me, and telling me I'm sweet won't help you, either."

"No, Kenny. I didn't mean any harm. I am very sorry that I did hurt you, but it was never planned...never."

"I don't believe you. I don't trust you. I trusted Bess. I gave her my heart and all those years--and look what it got me."

Pearl emitted a muffled sob. Kenny became even

more agitated and yanked her backwards. "At least this one didn't lie. But now, thanks to you, she's gonna be collateral damage."

Rose Ellen instinctively moved closer. It was what she would have done with anyone who was upset. Her efforts to ease the situation by stepping forward were met with even more rage.

"Don't come any closer, or you will find out what it feels like to be hurt. Before I kill you, though, I will slit Pearl's throat and you will watch her die. How's that for pain?"

A teardrop ran down Pearl's cheek as Rose Ellen tried again to reason with the knife wielding Kenny. "I'll do anything to make it up to you. What do you want me to do?"

Maybe, if she made him feel like she cared, he would drop the knife and let Pearl go, or just get distracted for a few seconds. Rose Ellen kept eyeing the door and tried to calculate how long it would take the two of them to flee.

"Like I said, it's too late. You know, I thought you were my last chance at love. We had a good time, and everything was going so well."

He gritted his teeth. "Then you decided that you wanted nothing to do with me, and that it was all over unless I wanted a relationship on YOUR terms. Well, I've turned the tables on you, haven't I? Just like I did with those others. Now, who's in control?"

Rose Ellen was afraid to ask for more details about the crimes, or Bess, but she had to. Whatever happened with Bess seemed to be a bleeding, open wound for Kenny, and was apparently connected to the homicides.

"Since we are both going to die anyway, Kenny, can you tell me what you mean about the others? What did you do?"

Perhaps her questions would provide some time to figure out how to escape. Rose Ellen remembered that on one of their regular crime shows, a victim had defused the situation by making the perpetrator feel like he was the center of attention. She accomplished that by asking the offender questions about himself.

It was important to make Kenny believe he was in total control. It might buy them a few more precious minutes. Rose Ellen felt like she was tottering on a strand of barbed wire stretched across a windy canyon. It seemed like there was no way to get to a safer place, and one false move meant she and Pearl were dead.

"I know it's too late for us, Kenny. But I can't say it enough. I am so sorry. Did the others hurt you, too?"

Kenny heaved. "I should have known they were going to stab me in the back, like Bess. You women are all the same."

He let out an evil cackle that sent chills up Rose Ellen's spine. "You went on that dating site for older adults to solicit women to kill?"

"Not at first. I mean, after I lost Bess, I wanted to give someone else a chance. I tried. I really did. I thought I would use the 'bad boy with a heart of gold' approach for my profile. Women like that, but it didn't make any difference."

"Women have it out for me. I do everything I can to please them and they do everything they can to destroy me. Three times! I gave those vixens a chance to prove me wrong. All three did the same thing. And then you...Did you know all of them had been married thirty-four years, like you? That's how long I had my Bess."

Kenny went on to explain that after a few dates, each woman quickly cut him off, refusing his phone calls and not answering his text messages.

Rose Ellen didn't dare verbalize it, but she could clearly see how Kenny would have turned women off with his constant pessimism and neediness.

But what did thirty-four years of marriage have to do with the seventeen dollars in cash left at the crime scenes?

She hesitated to push Kenny any further. Apparently, he had somehow been deeply hurt by his late wife. He attempted to rebound from that by finding other women to love. When they didn't respond to his romantic advances, he murdered them.

How sick, Rose Ellen thought, that a man would kill unsuspecting women as punishment for his wife's actions. But what had Bess done that was so horrible? Had she cheated on him and then died?

It was impossible to comprehend. A woman could not do anything terrible enough to turn a man into what seemed like a psychopathic serial killer. Not even adultery justified such evil. Only a twisted mind would kill three women because his wife had wronged him in some way.

There were so many things she wanted to ask the man holding a knife to her best friend's throat. But getting them out of there was the priority. What difference did the details make at this point, anyway?

Kenny started shifting his weight from one foot to the other. He was getting antsy. Another wave of panic swept over Rose Ellen. She had to come up with something fast. She was running out of time to save their lives.

I've got one more chance to try to get us out of this, Rose Ellen thought. She looked at the fear in Pearl's eyes and swallowed hard. "I know I don't deserve it, but are you sure you won't give me another chance, Kenny?"

She knew it was a long shot, but maybe he would buy that and drop the knife. Then she could grab Pearl's hand, and they would run faster than they had ever run in their lives.

"You don't deserve any more chances. I know your tricks. You are trying to make me give up and drop the knife. You think you can escape, don't you?"

"No, that's not it. It's just...well, I was afraid to take a chance on another relationship. But now I see that maybe things could work out between us."

"I'm not falling for that!" He pulled Pearl closer to him, and she winced as the knife dug deeper into her skin.

"You don't mean that at all. If I release you, the first thing you would do is run to the police and tell them everything. I can't let you do that."

Rose Ellen desperately tried to choke back her tears. "Okay. I know. This is it."

She closed her eyes and thought about what Heaven might look like and whether her dead parents would appear as she took her last breath. Would her life flash before her? Would she float above her own body as she lay dying?

It was heartbreaking to think that her daughter, Jennifer, would probably never be the same, and neither would Pearl's sons. Their murders would be devastating to so many people. It was bad enough that they were going to be killed, but even more horrible to think their murders, too, would probably go unsolved.

She opened her eyes and mouthed, "I love you" to Pearl. Tears began streaming down her best friend's face. And then Rose Ellen tried the last thing she could think of to keep them alive.

"The Lord is my shepherd, I shall not want; He makes me lie down in green pastures. He leads me beside still waters...."

Kenny abruptly turned toward the door, and Rose Ellen stopped her prayer in mid-sentence. Hope for their rescue soared when she heard what sounded like a car door slamming shut in her drive.

Confused by the interruption, Kenny frantically tried to decide what to do. He pushed Pearl forward and looked out the window.

Suddenly, the front door burst open, and chaos erupted like a prairie wildfire. Kenny lost his grip on the knife as the intruder lunged for him. Pearl broke free and quickly kicked his weapon under the coffee table. Oscar sailed from the couch like a gazelle and landed on Kenny's head. Rose Ellen desperately searched for her phone, spotted it on the table and quickly retrieved it.

Oscar tore into Kenny's flesh. He screamed, simultaneously grappling with the cat and trying to fend off the figure attacking him. He managed to pull Oscar off his face, and was instantly met with a giant blow that knocked him to his knees. Blood dripped down Kenny's cheek, and he clutched his chest and gasped for air.

"Nelda??" Rose Ellen was stunned to see her rival

repeatedly hitting Kenny in the head with one of her giant handbags.

Pearl jumped on his back and he hit the floor face down, as Nelda continued to pummel him. Rose Ellen shakily dialed 9-1-1.

"Give me something to tie this outlaw with!" Pearl screamed.

Rose Ellen grabbed a small table lamp as she cradled her cell phone next to her ear. She slammed the lamp down, and the base shattered as it hit the floor, loosening the cord. She put her foot on the base, and yanked the cord free with one hand, before throwing it to Pearl.

As Nelda continued to beat Kenny with her purse, Pearl pulled his arms back and quickly hogtied him.

Even in the middle of all the confusion, Rose Ellen wondered where Pearl had learned how to hogtie a person. She could ask that later, after help arrived and they were safe.

Pearl panted and asked, "Good grief, Nelda, what...what have you got in there?"

Kenny tried to lift his bloody head, but he only managed to moan as his face remained flat on the floor.

Nelda pulled a small handgun out of her suitcase of a handbag and pointed it at Kenny's bleeding temple.

"Move and I'll blow your miserable, cotton pickin' brains out!" she ordered.

Rose Ellen explained to the operator that they had captured a man who had just tried to kill her and Pearl. That man, she told the dispatcher, had confessed that he was the Seventeen Dollar Murderer.

Within minutes, cop cars and an ambulance came screaming up to Rose Ellen's lot. The first responders burst through the door. "Everybody freeze! Hands in the air!"

Nelda dropped her gun. "I couldn't let him kill them."

It didn't take long for the police to determine that the situation truly was what Rose Ellen had reported. Two witnesses had been on the verge of death. They had been rescued by an unexpected visitor. But why did Nelda just happen to show up?

"JDLR," Nelda told the officer in charge. "Some things just didn't look right, so I thought I'd better come check on Rose Ellen. I didn't know Pearl was here."

"You know about JDLR?" Rose Ellen looked surprised.

"Well, of course. I love Lieutenant Joe Kenda. He said that on one of his shows. I guess I just sensed things weren't right."

"I didn't know you liked those crime shows on the Investigation Discovery network."

"Doesn't everybody?" Nelda sniffed.

"So, this JDLR thing is the reason you dropped by?" The officer looked confused and scratched his head.

He gave the EMTs an affirmative nod as a stunned Kenny was untied and placed on a stretcher. "Surely, something else happened that prompted you to think there was a problem here tonight," the officer continued, as he turned his attention back to Nelda.

"Well-- first of all--it was weird when we had that fire at the Senior Society. I was close to the door, and I thought I was the first person out. But when I ran outside, I saw Kenny just calmly standing in the parking lot."

Nelda went on to explain that she noticed an open bathroom window. "As long as I've been going to the Senior Society, I've never seen that window open. In fact, I think it was locked on the inside. But that night, after I ran outside, I saw it was wide open, and it dawned on me that it was big enough for a person to fit through."

"Why didn't you say anything?"

"Well, sir, I just thought maybe Kenny had stepped out before the fire started or something, and maybe the window was opened because they had a smoke machine going inside. I kind of felt paranoid thinking Kenny might have started the fire and then climbed out the window."

The police officer was aware of the details surrounding the recent fire at the Monster Bash, but didn't realize that the open window was unusual.

"What else made you suspicious?" he asked.

"I know you won't take this seriously, but call it women's intuition. There was just something about the way Kenny looked at Rose Ellen that bothered me. One minute he would stare at her like she hung the moon and then...I don't know how to explain it. His facial expression would just change. It was like a dark, evil look came over him."

Rose Ellen had not picked up on that at all and shook her head. Pearl grimaced, as if to say "Me, neither. I never saw the diabolical, Mr. Hyde side."

"It's like they say on our crime shows," Nelda added. "Evil people often get in the red zone, and to me, sometimes Kenny looked like he was on the edge of plunging past that point of no return."

"I understand why you wondered about the open window, and the fact that it appeared he may have quickly exited the building after possibly starting the fire, but that's not a lot," said the officer, ignoring her other comments. "Was there something else that made you feel like it was important to come here tonight?"

There was something else, Nelda explained— something that had happened just before she decided to arrive unannounced at Rose Ellen's home.

Nelda had briefly stopped at a hardware store just before dark to pick up paper towels they had on sale. She spotted Kenny ahead of her, approached him from behind, and noticed the contents of his basket.

"It had things like rope, duct tape, a box of latex gloves and several plastic tarps in it. I thought that was strange, particularly since it was late in the day. Do you know anybody our age that would buy things like that? And most people we know don't do that much shopping when it is getting dark."

"As I was saying," she continued, "on the real-life crime shows they emphasize that even if you have no proof, you need to worry about things that just don't look right. And that REALLY didn't look right. Like I said before-- JDLR."

Nelda went on to describe how she had quickly stepped into the next aisle, so he wouldn't see her. She thought Kenny's purchases were very suspicious but still, it didn't mean he was going to commit a homicide, or that he was the Seventeen Dollar Murderer.

"I got home and I just couldn't shake the idea that

something was wrong. I kept telling myself it was crazy to think Kenny could be a criminal, but with the murders happening, and the fire and the stuff I saw him buying…well, paranoid or not, I just decided to drop in on Rose Ellen. I knew he had been spending a lot of time with her lately."

Nelda glanced at Rose Ellen and continued, "I know we are not exactly friends, but I felt like it was my obligation to see if you were okay."

"It's a good thing you did," the officer responded. "I think we have enough information for now. We may call you down to the station sometime later. You ladies just try to get some rest. Are you sure no one is hurt?"

"We're fine," Pearl answered, rubbing her neck. "He didn't manage to really cut me, thank goodness." She turned to Nelda. "I never understood why you carried those gigantic handbags, but I am so grateful you had one tonight."

"Yes," echoed Rose Ellen. "I'm glad it was heavy, too. That gun inside probably helped put a few dents in his head. Thanks for saving our lives, Nelda. And Pearl…you and your lipstick…that helped, too. What if you hadn't seen Kenny coming? I might be dead right now. I won't ever fuss at you again about checking your lipstick in the mirror. We are all okay because of you two."

Oscar let out a high pitched "Meow," and looked up at Rose Ellen, like he was asking, "Hey, what about me? Don't you think I played a part in this rescue?"

She stroked his back and gave him a kiss on the head. "Yes, Oscar. You saved us, too. I'm so proud of you. What a good boy!"

Physically, they were fine, but the events from the

past few months had been emotionally devastating, particularly their brush with death. They could have been his next victims. Rose Ellen thought about the other women and wondered how many people's lives had been changed forever because of Kenny's violent acts.

She closed her eyes and said a silent prayer of thanks. They were alive, and she was grateful for that. But there were so many puzzling questions. How could someone they had spent time with murder three women and leave them each holding seventeen dollars? And what did that mean?

How could he start a fire at the Senior Society? He could have killed everyone inside. Did Kenny just fake having a good time at the Monster Bash? Was he a sociopath? He seemed so thrilled to win the costume contest. What went wrong?

Rose Ellen had tried to befriend him. Why would he turn on her and then want to make her his fourth homicide victim? Nothing made any sense. Apparently, a seemingly normal person in their midst was a homicidal maniac.

Eleven

It was all in Kenny's ten-page confession that he feverishly scribbled on a large, yellow note pad. He described his crimes in graphic detail, from a straight-backed chair in a small, dark interview room, known as "the box" at the Tyler Police Station.

After being checked out at the hospital, it was determined that Kenny had only suffered a few bumps, cuts and bruises. The narcissistic killer was more than willing to confess verbally, elaborate about all the gory details on paper, and brag about his evil deeds.

First, Bess was not dead. She might as well be, he wrote. Bess had left him for another man after thirty-four years of marriage.

In Kenny's rambling confession, he said that they had married young, had children right away and for years, everything seemed good. Like most couples, they concentrated on making a living and raising their children. Then, he wrote, things changed.

What else could I do? I worked hard. I allowed Bess to have what she needed, if it was truly necessary. We had a nice, little house and enough to eat. And then she up and announced that she wasn't happy. What? After thirty-four years, she decided that she didn't love me and was leaving me for someone she had fallen in love with. I asked her why. She said that when the children were pretty much raised, she discovered that we had lost our relationship somewhere along the way.

Lost our relationship? I gave her an allowance

and took her out to eat every year on her birthday. What else did Bess want? I remember when she kept nagging me about taking dance lessons. I told her she was nuts. We were too old to do that and besides—I was tired on the weekends. I just wanted to sit and watch my ballgames. After all, a man is the king of his castle. Why couldn't she remember that?

Bess didn't try to understand that her job—after the kids became independent-- was to focus on me. What kind of a woman would just up and decide to pack her bags? She claimed that she had warned me over and over that our marriage was in trouble. She said I never listened to her, or cared about her problems. What problems? I gave her the perfect life.

Oh, sure. She said she had told me for years that we needed to go to counseling. But that is just for crazy people. I asked her how she could say our love had died. And you know what she said to me? 'Our love's not dead, Kenny. It's just buried alive.' Bess claimed, that for the last seventeen years of our marriage, she had been begging me to revive our relationship. Dance lessons, letting her whine about her feelings and counseling? That was ridiculous. The only thing wrong with us—was her! When I told her that, she walked out the door.

Seventeen years. When the interrogator read that, he did a double take. "So, she felt the last seventeen years of your marriage were not happy?"

Kenny looked up at him and gritted his teeth. "Bess said the first seventeen were pretty good, but that she wouldn't give me dollar for each of the last seventeen years we were together. Can you believe that? How ungrateful and disloyal."

Detective Paul Peterson was stunned. "Is that why you left each victim holding seventeen dollars in cash?"

"It's all in there!" Kenny pointed to the yellow pad that he had turned over to the officer. "Keep on reading!"

As the detective scanned the confession, Kenny started to cry. "She didn't appreciate me. I loved her. I gave her so much. I can't hate her, though. I just can't..."

"Did you kill her, too?"

"No. She just left and said she would send me the divorce papers. I moved here to Tyler, and let her know that we could pick up where we left off. I was certain she would eventually come to her senses, realize her mistake and comprehend the fact that I was the most important thing in her life."

He took a deep breath and continued, "I thought she would come crawling back, focus her attention on me and try to make up for her sins. I never dreamed she would go through with the divorce, but the papers finally came from some two-bit lawyer, and I had no choice, but to sign them."

"So, she never tried to reconcile with you?"

Kenny put his head in his hands. "No. She never came back to me. She...she chose to stay with that...that other man. How could she get involved with someone while we were married? Why would Bess want to be with him when she had me? She was a liar and a cheat. I didn't need that, so I decided I could move on with someone else, too."

"Why did you kill the others?"

"They were the same. I met them online on that

dating site. All three of them acted like things were good, and we could be happy like Bess and me. Then, they all deceived me and turned their backs on me, too."

Detective Peterson stepped out of the interrogation room and spoke to the officer on the other side of the one-way mirror.

"I think we have a case here of rage displacement. He moved his anger from the actual target—the wife who left him—to targets that he felt were safer."

"You are right. Our suspect couldn't bring himself to kill his wife for leaving him, so he transferred his rage to targets that he could punish without feeling as guilty. He didn't have as much invested in them emotionally, but in his mind, they left him, too. It's sick. There's no doubt about that. But it happens, and more often than we'd like to admit," the officer replied.

There was no justification for what Kenny had done, but unfortunately something in his twisted mind made him decide to punish three women. He felt they deserved the ultimate penalty because they had betrayed him, like his wife did.

"Good job, Peterson," the officer said. "You still know exactly how to deal with a scumbag in the box. Once again, you managed to get a suspect to open up."

"Thanks. I'll see what else he has to say."

Detective Peterson finished reading the confession and re-entered the room. "I understand now what the significance of the seventeen dollars was. You thought because they had all been married thirty-four years like you and Bess--that maybe they felt the last seventeen years of their marriages had been miserable, right?"

"They were just like Bess. Even though they weren't divorced, they probably hated the last seventeen years of their marriages, too. I mean, I knew when each one of them said how long they had been married, it was a sign."

"A sign? Did any of the women actually tell you that the last seventeen years of their marriages had been terrible?"

"No. They didn't have to. I knew how they felt. I could tell. They left me right away after just a few dates. They probably rejected their poor husbands too, just like what Bess did to me. I bet they had all committed adultery."

Somehow in Kenny's perverted version of reality, he made that assumption. What a strange leap, thought the detective, to decide just because a woman had been married the same number of years she felt like Bess did—that the last seventeen years of matrimony had been unhappy.

On top of that distorted presumption, being rejected by the three women apparently had pushed Kenny completely over the edge—into that deep, dark hole of depravity.

"I put the money in their selfish hands after I killed them. That's what they get—a dollar for each miserable year, just like Bess said."

The detective shook his head in disbelief and scanned the written confession again. "Let's go over why there wasn't any DNA at the crime scenes. How did you manage that?"

"I told you!" Kenny screamed. "It's all in there!"

"I know, and you did tell us the basics about the crimes, but I'd like to hear more details from someone who managed to be as clever as you."

Detective Peterson used a method he had found effective in the past—make the perpetrator feel in control. It worked well with narcissistic killers—lie and give them a false sense of bravado. He wanted Kenny to think he was brilliant to commit crimes that he almost got away with.

Kenny gave the detective an evil smile. "That was easy. I killed them at my house. I wore a wig and used latex gloves. I was really careful when I stabbed them, so I wouldn't cut myself and get my blood on them. But that wasn't too hard, since they were already gone when I slit their throats."

He went on to explain that he put on coveralls and shoe protectors before he took them to the locations where he dumped their bodies. There was no significance, he said, about the locations except for the fact that he picked places that were fairly isolated.

He had spent months selecting the locations to dump his victims. The boarded-up Foley's store, the abandoned Walmart and the field just outside of town all had the same things in common. They were in less traveled areas and none had working surveillance cameras.

"How did you get them to come to your house? I don't see that in your confession."

"That wasn't as easy. But I used the helpless routine. I called each one of them and cried. I said I was going to kill myself if they didn't come over. Women are stupid fixers, so it worked—even after they said they didn't want to see me again."

He grinned with delight as he recalled his diabolical plot. "And I got away with it because they didn't know about each other. They were just women I had met on the dating site. Who would suspect a poor, old widower like me would end up killing them?"

"Is that why you lied about your marital status? To gain sympathy from these women?"

"Yes," Kenny replied. "And trust. The 'poor me' routine makes women trust you."

He added some gruesome details, like the fact that he used the ploy of telling the women that the sleeping pills he planned to use for his suicide were on the bedside table.

They had all reacted exactly as he thought they would. They immediately wanted to help Kenny by retrieving and destroying the pills. His depraved scheme, unfortunately, was successful three different times.

As they entered his bedroom, Kenny followed. He hurriedly put on the wig and gloves and slipped up behind each woman. He used the rope to choke the life out of all three victims. Taken completely by surprise, none even had a chance to scream for help.

Then he changed into his coveralls, meticulously placed the women on tarps and viciously stabbed them. The overkill was motivated by his intense hatred, and the fact that he "really wanted to mess them up and confuse the police."

The only thing really messed up and confused, thought Detective Peterson, was Kenny. It was hard to imagine someone stabbing a person who was already dead.

Kenny wrapped the bodies in the tarps they lay on, careful to duct tape them closed. He slipped to the dump sights late at night. If anyone happened to see him, they would probably think he was just carrying something large and bulky, like a rug.

But no one spotted him in the dark as he loaded the bodies in his trunk, or at the remote areas he had chosen for the victims' final resting places. He said he wasn't really concerned about the bodies being discovered. Kenny felt sure he had left no evidence that could be traced back to him.

New supplies were purchased for each crime. After every homicide, the rope, gloves, duct tape, coveralls, shoe protectors and wig he used were tossed into various dumpsters along his route home. And then, Kenny glibly remarked, each time he made one more stop before returning to the Tiny House Village. He went to his favorite fast food restaurant and ordered a hamburger, large chocolate milkshake and fries.

The seasoned officer had faced a lot of devious criminals, but he considered Kenny a horrific psychopath, at the very least. Much like Ted Bundy, he had no remorse and had used helplessness and a "nice guy" facade to trap unsuspecting victims into a murderous, deceitful web.

He bragged to Detective Peterson that, "I would have easily gotten away with a few more murders, if it hadn't been for that stupid Nelda. If I had known she was coming to Rose Ellen's house, I could have ended up eliminating six women. She messed up everything!"

Paul Peterson let out a sigh of relief. Nelda's actions stopped a serial killer in his tracks—a nefarious one whose target was baby boomer women.

Why Kenny set the Senior Society on fire was still a mystery. When pressed by the detective, Kenny explained that he felt the Seventeen Dollar Murder cases were "too hot." He thought the fire might divert attention—at least for a while—from the homicides.

Nelda's suspicion about Kenny's behavior at the Monster Bash was right on target. He had gone into the bathroom, started a fire in the trash bin and then unlocked the window. He climbed out and waited in the parking lot. His plan was to hide and then blend into the crowd, but Nelda had emerged from the Senior Society building before he could execute his vicious plot.

There was another reason Kenny had attacked the Senior Society, and it went along with his feelings of rage displacement. As his anger and resentment festered, he began to think that everyone was responsible for his unhappiness.

Murdering three women was not enough, it seemed. Their deaths just fueled the fire burning in his sick mind. He decided that the whole world was after him—even the men and women at the Senior Society.

"But you won the costume contest. From what I understand, everyone was happy for you, weren't they?" Detective Peterson wondered aloud.

"It was all fake. No one really cares about you. I thought they were happy for me, until I saw the hypocrisy on their faces. They were all out there thinking about how they could ruin me. You can't trust anyone. Just look how I trusted Bess and the other women. Rose Ellen acted like she wanted to be with me, too. Everyone is a liar. I gave and gave, and each time I was the one that got taken. It was time to make people pay."

Even for a seasoned detective who felt like he had seen everything, hearing such a wicked confession was too much. Nothing Kenny said was the least bit logical. He had lost any moral compass he may have had and all sense of reason.

Experts could say that Kenny had antisocial personality disorder, or label him a psychopath or sociopath. It didn't matter, thought Detective Peterson. The cold, hard truth was all that really mattered.

Kenny was a calculating, self-involved killer who destroyed other people with his evil manipulation. No punishment would be severe enough for such an ultimate, revolting control freak.

The detective finished the interview and emerged from the claustrophobic room where he had come face to face with an unbelievably horrible monster.

Rose Ellen, Nelda and Pearl had been summoned to the station. Detective Peterson felt he owed them the full explanation for what Kenny had done—and for what he had attempted to do, even though it was impossible to really explain such horrendous acts.

The women sat stunned as the detective went over the sordid details about Kenny's crimes and his strange justification for them.

"It was true, Pearl. The murderer was hiding in plain sight," Rose Ellen sighed.

"Like they say on our crime shows on the Investigation Discovery network, monsters are often impossible to spot, even when they have been right in front of you all along. Remember that one guy? He was supposedly happily married and a deacon in his church. No one close to him had a clue that he had killed a bunch of people," Pearl added. "But somehow, you saw Kenny for what he was, Nelda."

"Not really. I just had a nagging feeling that

something wasn't right. I felt it wouldn't hurt to see if Rose Ellen was okay. I thought I was probably being paranoid, but it seemed worth the effort."

"All I can say, Nelda, is that you earned more than a few stars in your crown. You deserve a big, diamond tiara. What you did was really heroic."

After all they had been through, it was strange for Rose Ellen to hear those words come out of her mouth. She had to acknowledge the fact that an archrival not only cared enough to check on her--Nelda had also saved her life.

Rose Ellen took a deep breath and uttered the phrase she never thought she would say to her nemesis. "Maybe it's time for us to bury the hatchet."

"Yes," Nelda replied. "I guess I've come to that place in my life. I feel like I need to look at things more positively, now. I have to stop being jealous of you."

"What? Jealous of me? Why?"

"From way back, you always had everything I wanted. You were cute, smart, you had a hot guy in high school. Everybody liked you. I was always kind of a strange outsider."

"I never thought of you that way," Rose Ellen said.

"Really? That's why I learned to be flamboyant. That way, at least I wasn't invisible. People gravitated to you. But me—well, I had to make people notice me. And men never chased me, like they did you. I had to chase them."

Rose Ellen's heart ached for her former rival. She never realized Nelda felt left out in high school. There were the usual cliques, and Nelda was always a bit different. Maybe she hadn't been part of the so-called "in crowd," but Rose Ellen didn't understand at the time, that Nelda's sometimes outrageous behavior was based on her feelings of inadequacy.

"You two should have talked this over years ago," Pearl declared.

It was true, thought Rose Ellen. The rift between them could have, and should have, been mended before it became such an enormous fracture. It was childish, particularly now that they were seniors. It was time to put on their big girl panties and move forward.

Rose Ellen reached out and hugged Nelda. It felt good to forgive, she thought. Life was too short as it was. At their ages, life was getting shorter, and wasting even one more minute on mounting bitterness and misunderstandings from the past was useless.

Nelda gave Rose Ellen a gentle squeeze and apologetically whispered, "I'm sorry for everything."

"Me, too."

Detective Peterson looked the other way, adjusted his cowboy hat and shuffled his feet to avoid being drawn into the heart-to heart "girl talk."

"Thank you again, Nelda, for caring enough to come to my house. You truly did save us from a horrible fate. We never saw it coming, that is for sure," Rose Ellen said, with a heavy sigh.

"I guess we weren't such great detectives, were we?" Pearl asked. "We are boomer/seniors who couldn't unravel a murder mystery that involved women from our generation, right here in Tyler."

"We gave it a shot, and that's what's important. You had some great ideas, and it was interesting to try to get to the bottom of the Seventeen Dollar Murders," responded Rose Ellen.

"And now—who knows? You might end up taking some classes at Tyler Junior College, and that could open a whole, new world for you. So at least a few small, good things came out of a very bad situation. I just wish I knew what to do for the families of the victims. It's so sad to think about what they have been through, and the agony they will face as they deal with their grief."

Detective Peterson jumped on the chance to interrupt. "Actually, there is something you can do. We have a victims' rights organization that helps people who have either lost loved ones to violent crimes, or were survivors of something awful. They do counseling and act as a support group."

"Really? But I don't have a degree in psychology or anything. I'm not a counselor, and I don't know what it is like to lose someone to murder."

"No," said the detective, "but you do know what it's like to be a victim of a violent crime. You could help those people who may have survived and are having difficulty dealing with emotions, like survivors' guilt. We have training classes for our volunteers. You would be surprised at how many people go through a lot of guilt when they lose someone to violence."

Rose Ellen asked, "I guess like a 'why them and not me' thing, right?"

"Yes. People who have suffered that kind of a loss need all the help they can get. You could make a difference for them."

"I read that F. Scott Fitzgerald said it's never too late to be what you want to be," Nelda added. "And I think somebody else famous said something about how we are never too old to set another goal, or dream a new dream."

Rose Ellen nodded in agreement, a bit surprised that Nelda sounded intelligent when she spoke without using her baby voice.

Before marriage and motherhood, Rose Ellen had considered doing something to help crime victims. How satisfying it would be, she thought, to finally chase a long-ignored dream.

"Can you get me more information about that victims' rights program?"

"I'll be happy to. I'm officially retired, but I do assist them with interviews here, occasionally, on a contract basis. That was my specialty when I was on the force. I'm here at this station quite a bit, so I can help you sign up for the next class, if you would like."

"That would be great."

Rose Ellen had noticed that Detective Peterson seemed a bit older than the other officers there. He had beautiful, silver hair and a craggy face that reflected his years of experience. She was also aware of the fact that his deep, blue eyes were fixed on Nelda.

"You dress so nicely, Nelda," Detective Peterson awkwardly commented.

She let out a silly giggle, and Rose Ellen couldn't help but flinch a bit. Nelda had her usual too short, too tight outfit on, and was donning another "big hair," blonde wig that matched her giant handbag. But it was obvious that Detective Peterson was quite taken with her signature look.

"You know, you have the same pretty, blue eyes that Joe Kenda has, and I bet you have solved as many cases, too," Nelda said, reverting to her baby voice.

"Oh, no. I've successfully wrapped up my share of murder cases, but I can't say I've solved over three hundred like the *Homicide Hunter,*" Detective Peterson nervously replied. "But thank you for the compliments, just the same."

Nelda shifted her weight so that her breasts and hips would be more noticeable, and looked down at Detective Peterson's left hand. Her eyes lit up when she did not see a wedding ring.

"Well, ladies, I think we are finished here. Just for the record...um...are you married?" he asked, never bothering to look at Pearl or Rose Ellen.

Nelda winked and instantly answered, "I'm not, Detective Peterson."

"You can call me Paul," he said. "Me, neither. Would you like to get a cup of coffee or something...sometime?"

"Of course," Nelda said, flashing her best, flirty look. "The 'or something' sounds particularly intriguing, Paul. How about now?"

Detective Peterson's rugged face turned a deep shade of red as he sheepishly reached for Nelda's hand. "Well, I guess that would be okay. My part is done, and Kenny is in good hands. The other fellows can take it from here, and everyone involved will make sure he gets what's coming to him."

It was over. There would be no more Seventeen Dollar Murders. But for the families and friends of each victim, it would never be over. Rose Ellen made a silent vow. She would do her best to become someone who could help people dealing with tragic losses.

"Nelda, we can head over to IHOP," said the detective. "I have a Harley Trike out front and an extra helmet. Would you like a ride?"

"Oh, yes!" she replied. "I have always wanted to take one of those bad boys for a spin, and I know I'll be perfectly safe with my arms around you, Paul."

As they walked away together, Pearl sighed. "It looks like we've found that good things can come out of even the worst situations."

"Yes. We learned a lot about each other. By the way, Pearl. I never knew you could hogtie someone. Where did you pick that up?"

"Oh, Ex. Even after all these years, there are some things you don't know about me," Pearl said with a mischievous grin.

Rose Ellen smiled. "Now, thankfully, we have more time to enjoy our friendship and discover new things about each other."

"Yes, thank God," Pearl sighed. "I'm glad we made it."

"I think it's great that Nelda and I mended a fence, too. It also seems like we all have a chance to chase our dreams before it's too late to catch them. Maybe it's never too late to still be productive and help other people. I'm just so sorry that three women are dead."

"I know. Theirs dreams died with them. Maybe the best way to honor them is to remember that we are more than capable of contributing to society, and we should do that as long as we possibly can," Pearl added.

"That's true," Rose Ellen agreed. "Like Detective Peterson said, boomer/seniors like us can still make a difference. And we certainly didn't get this old by being stupid, did we?"

"I guess we also found out that Nelda can be over

the top sometimes, and she pushes the envelope way too far, that's for sure. But deep down inside, she does have a good heart. Maybe she could mend a fence with Ruth, too."

"Time will tell," Rose Ellen responded. "But for now, let's just appreciate the fact that we lived to see another day, and we have hope for tomorrow."

"Amen."

They saw Detective Peterson slide his arm around Nelda's waist as they strolled down the long hallway leading to the police station's main entrance. She looked back over her shoulder and beamed at Pearl and Rose Ellen.

"I guess we have also learned that you don't always have to cast a wide net, or even bait your hook to get what you want. Sometimes you get lucky, and that trophy just jumps right in your boat," Rose Ellen said with a laugh.

"Oh, that is so true, Ex. The way things look from here, Nelda may be through chasing that dream she was always trying to catch. I think she finally landed the big one."

About Melinda Richarz Lyons

Melinda Richarz Lyons earned a B.A. in Journalism from the University of North Texas and has been a free lance writer for over forty years. Her articles have appeared in many publications, including *Nashville Parent, Cats Magazine, True West, Chicken Soup for the Soul: True Love, Kids, Etc., Frontier Times, Reminisce, Cincinnati Family Magazine, Small Town Kids* and *Chicken Soup for the Soul: Grandmothers.*

An award-winning songwriter, she has also authored several books including the young readers novel, *Murder at the Oaklands Mansion,* and a romance/mystery, *Heir to a Secret.* Her non-fiction grief book, *Crossing the Minefield,* garnered a Royal Palm Literary Award and is included in grief support programs and bereavement library collections in all fifty states, including the Patient/Family Library at the MD Anderson Cancer Center.

In addition, Ms. Lyons regularly contributes to various grief and senior websites and speaks to organizations and schools about the craft of writing. All her books are available in both Kindle and paperback forms on www.amazon.com. She lives in Tyler, Texas and invites you to visit her website: www.melindalyons.weebly.com.

Made in the USA
Lexington, KY
07 September 2018